7/08

DEC 05

DATE DUE

SEP 19

KILLER'S
RANGE

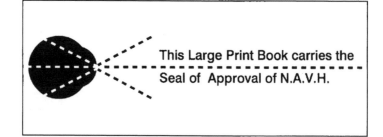

This Large Print Book carries the
Seal of Approval of N.A.V.H.

KILLER'S RANGE

Chet Cunningham

Thorndike Press • Waterville, Maine

Published in 2005 by arrangement with Chet Cunningham.

Thorndike Press® Large Print Western.

The tree indicium is a trademark of Thorndike Press.

The text of this Large Print edition is unabridged.
Other aspects of the book may vary from the original edition.

Set in 16 pt. Plantin by Minnie B. Raven.

Printed in the United States on permanent paper.

Library of Congress Cataloging-in-Publication Data

Cunningham, Chet.
    Killer's range / by Chet Cunningham.
        p. cm. — (Thorndike Press large print westerns)
    ISBN 0-7862-7985-0 (lg. print : hc : alk. paper)
    1. Ranchers — Fiction. 2. Kansas — Fiction.
3. Large type books. I. Title. II. Thorndike Press large
print Western series.
PS3553.U468K55 2005
    813'.54—dc22   2005016541

KILLER'S RANGE

As the Founder/CEO of NAVH, the only national health agency solely devoted to those who, although not totally blind, have an eye disease which could lead to serious visual impairment, I am pleased to recognize Thorndike Press★ as one of the leading publishers in the large print field.

Founded in 1954 in San Francisco to prepare large print textbooks for partially seeing children, NAVH became the pioneer and standard setting agency in the preparation of large type.

Today, those publishers who meet our standards carry the prestigious "Seal of Approval" indicating high quality large print. We are delighted that Thorndike Press is one of the publishers whose titles meet these standards. We are also pleased to recognize the significant contribution Thorndike Press is making in this important and growing field.

Lorraine H. Marchi, L.H.D.
Founder/CEO
NAVH

★ Thorndike Press encompasses the following imprints: Thorndike, Wheeler, Walker and Large Print Press.

Chapter One

The warming April sun touched the low range of hills to the west, toyed with the ridge for a moment, and melted into it, inching its crimson circle lower until the dusky haze turned the glow to a deep purple before it dropped from sight. Jed Hart rode on steadily, searching six-year-old memories.

He came toward the little town from the west. Somehow, it seemed there were fewer ranches in the valley than when he had ridden away to help preserve the Union. But now it was 1870, and he was coming home to stay.

The sorrel topped a small rise, and Jed brought her to a halt. Yes, this was familiar — Sein Creek. It meandered from the low ridges behind him into Hendersonville. The stream stirred many happy memories for him. The trail sloped gently to the river from the rise and joined the stage road, which disappeared into a cluster of willow and ash where the trail met the creek.

"Buckets Crossing," Jed said out loud. The reason for the name had long been forgotten, but the name stuck. It was four miles to Hendersonville from the crossing. Jed swung out of the saddle, and as he flexed his trail-weary legs, his horse began to search for spring grass. Jed knuckled the low-crowned, black Stetson back on his head and drew his sleeve across his tanned forehead. It was six years since he had ridden down the streets of his hometown, since he had seen his parents. Did he really want to go back?

He squatted in the dust of the trail and drew lines with a stick. Yes, he did want to go home. He had drifted long enough. It was time he tried to do something more than simply live from one sunset to the next. He wondered what had happened to his parents.

Jed stepped into the stirrup and pulled himself up. But his mind drifted back to the small cattle spread his dad had worked. What would the place look like now?

A new sensation crowded into his memories until he was fully aware of it. A horse pounded down the hard-packed stage road somewhere ahead. He could not see anyone; they must be beyond the trees.

Jed pulled the sorrel to a stop and listened. The sound of the hoofs slowed, but came closer. Then they slowed again and stopped. Jed's pale-blue eyes squinted slightly at the area below before he urged the horse ahead at a walk. His senses told him there was no danger. After eighteen months of leading patrols and living or dying on the keen edge of his senses, he had developed a quick awareness of danger. He felt none now.

The approaching rider could have stopped at the creek for several reasons. Jed kept the sorrel at a walk as he gained the stage road and turned left toward the ford. The bulk of the trees clustered this side of the stream, and the dark coolness seemed inviting. The cover was not as thick as it appeared, and Jed relaxed his right hand at his side. His six-gun in its holster was tied lower than most cowpokes would carry it.

He made no attempt to come in quietly, and as he rounded a scattering of brush, a movement upstream caught his attention. A horse stood, head down, munching on the spring grass that had pushed up from the wash of new topsoil. Near the horse, a gray-haired man huddled over some wood, trying to blow it into a fire. The old man had apparently not heard Jed approach and continued tinkering with the fire. Jed walked his horse up close. The younger man sat in the saddle and rolled a cigarette. He lit the smoke, then flipped the small firebrand away.

"Well fer kittenfish sakes, stranger, don't just sit there!" the old man said without looking around. "You could give me a hand so we kin get a fire a going and get some coffee hot."

Jed dropped off the sorrel and walked to the edge of the stream. He found the high-water mark where the spring surge had deposited a wealth of sticks and twigs. They were tinder-dry now and ready to burn. He gathered an armload and carried it back to the fire. Slowly, he fed the twigs into the tiny fire until it grew into a respectable cooking fire.

The old man stood and slapped his thigh with his battered, high-crowned hat.

"So that's how to make a fire — hunt up dry wood. Never could make a campfire. Oh, I make fires up to my place, but truth is I slosh 'bout half a cup of corn on them first, and then she burns to a fair-you-well!"

Jed sat back from the fire and looked at the other man.

"You said something about coffee?"

"That's so, that's so!" He fumbled at his saddle and took off a gunny sack, which he shook out on the ground.

Jed tried to fit the man into a type. He was not a saddle bum — too old for general range work. He had to be a local since he was not rigged for long riding. Jed figured the man was over sixty years old. He wore his hair long and his beard the same way. Both were gray now, a dark-tinged color that Jed suspected was mostly dirt. Jed guessed the smaller man was five feet four. He wore broadcloth suit pants that had seen regular pressing at one time and a cotton flannel shirt with a leather vest over it. A red kerchief knotted around his throat. The old man was as trail-dirty as the last rider pushing a summer herd.

The old-timer found what he wanted in the pile on the ground and took the quart-sized can to the creek for coffee water. Back at the fire, he arranged two stones carefully and set the can over them, edging it into the glow of coals. Reaching under his saddle, he pulled out a jug with a corncob stopper. He held it up by its crockery handle.

"Like a dust-chasing swaller of corn, friend?" Before Jed could answer, the other

11

man pulled the cob out and tilted the brown container to his lips.

Jed reached for the jug when the other offered it. The liquid clawed at his throat. It was corn all right, home-mash corn whiskey with a kick like a gun-shy stallion.

The old man slapped his leg and laughed.

"Been a long time since you had any fresh corn, I'll bet a ninny! Least you can take it. Never trust a man who won't drink my corn." He put the cob back in the jug and set it by his saddle. The old man's eyes were close-set and dark. Now they danced with sudden mirth, and his smile broke quickly. A ragged rank of black stumps showed where his teeth once were. He tossed his hat on the ground as he leaned back.

"Didn't see you in town, young feller, so you must be coming in." He paused, but Jed said nothing. "Not a big talker, are you? Well, dang it, got to be a few good listeners." He leaned over and held out his hand.

"Name's McIntosh, Corn McIntosh. I'm well known in these parts."

Jed took the hand, surprised at the hard grip.

"Folks call me Jed. That corn of yours is the real stuff."

"Knew you'd be a body that'd like good

corn." His eyes crinkled again, and Jed knew he had a good start toward making a friend. Corn untied the blanket from his saddle and dug out a can of beans and some hard biscuits.

"I'm sleeping over here tonight, Jed. Something about that boarding house and hotel that gives me the jitters. Only about four miles into town, you care to ride."

"Hadn't decided, Corn. Mind if I share your fire?" The old man shook his head, and Jed moved to the sorrel and loosened the saddle cinch before he took a flour sack from one of the saddlebags. It held what was left of his food. He had some strips of jerky, hard crackers and a handful of dried fruit a rancher's wife had given him two days ago. Jed put the fruit into a can filled with water and set it on the coals. He chewed on the jerky and ate the crackers.

"From looks of you," Corn said, sizing him up, "I'd say you was lookin' for a straight riding job. None of this cutting wood or fixing the barn roof or making corrals. Straight wrangling man!"

"Could be," Jed nodded. "What's this little town like? Cow town?"

Corn snorted. "Sure it's cow town. This is Kansas, boy, and the Arkansas River

Valley. This is all cow town around here, always will be. Where you from? Texas?" He hurried on. "Naw, not mean-lookin' enough. We got one big outfit here, the Slash S, and it's on the prod to shove the little ranchers out of the county. Can't do it legal, but they got other ways."

"What's the town like? How many people?" Jed asked to prime the old man.

"People? Too danged many! It ain't no St. Louis, but maybe 300 souls in the county. Town's got three bars, one-half a hotel, six or seven stores, and a livery stable. Had a bank till last year when some varmint robbed it and busted half the county. Now folks hold onto their gold. Got a schoolhouse and a circuit preacher. We don't see him but once ever' two months."

"What about a marshal?"

"You guys with a tied-down gun always ask." Corn tested the coffee and put it back to boil some more. "Sure we got a town marshal. You might as well gun him down as anybody. He got hired last year. His handle's Paul Partlow, and he's the brother of the Partlows who run the Slash S." Corn snorted. "Some marshal. He couldn't hit an outhouse when he was inside it!"

14

Jed motioned at Corn's gun. "Notice your six-gun has a tie-down strap across the hammer. Not exactly a fast-draw outfit."

"Boy, you got to stop readin' them dime novels. Only reason I got this forty-four is rattlesnakes and coyotes. Don't reckon I got to be fast on the draw for them. Now you want some coffee, or don't ya?"

Jed laughed and reached for a tin-can cup that Corn offered. He liked this snaggle-toothed old character. Corn knew the lay of the land in Hendersonville; Jed did not. He could find out more in an hour with Corn than in a day prowling around town.

As they ate, darkness closed in; Jed built up the fire. It felt good in the chill of the starry night. He had decided to stay over. Corn dug out the jug again, and they passed it back and forth. Corn told him a lot about the town he already knew. Then the old-timer pointed his finger at Jed.

"Almost forgot the latest news. Rancher got himself shot on a little place out near the foothills. Lived long enough to ride back to his woman. Told her the name of the guy who gunned him. He said the killer was Jed Hart."

Jed watched Corn carefully, but he was

not joking. Nor was he watching Jed for a reaction. Corn had simply passed on some news.

"Another rancher got himself shot like that two, three months ago. Nobody knew who did it for sure. Musta been this Hart, too. His mother lives in town. Funny, though, far as anybody knows, Jed Hart died in a cavalry charge under Sheridan at Nineveh."

Chapter Two

Jed sipped the bitter coffee slowly. So his mother thought he was dead. Nineveh had been a confused battle. He had taken a rifle ball, and his name must have gone on the killed list instead of the wounded. Word got back to his parents, and when he never came home . . .

Now some killer was using his name. Why? Why after six years?

Jed tossed more wood on the fire and drained the last of the coffee from his cup. He looked at the older man.

"Corn, I might as well bed down here."

The old-timer nodded and rolled out his blanket. He lay on it with his feet aimed at the fire. The corn whiskey and the riding had drained his strength.

Jed lay under his blanket for a long time watching the fire die to an even red glow. His mind was a jumble of questions he had to have answered. Why was his mother living in town? Why hadn't Corn mentioned his father? And who was the killer using his name? The questions nagged at him until he fell asleep.

The chatter of a red-winged blackbird calling its mate woke Jed at dawn. He rolled out of the blanket and kindled a fire. The evening chill washed away with the sun that spun over the low hills to the east and blossomed into a Kansas sunflower.

Corn McIntosh roused out of his blanket and washed the sleep from his eyes in the creek. The old man produced a battered iron skillet and some eggs, but Jed shook his head.

"I need a ride to clear my head, Corn. Then I got business in town."

Corn pulled at his beard, and his eyes flashed as he came over to shake hands with Jed as he finished saddling the sorrel.

"None of my business, but I like to have front and back names for folks — specially folks who like good corn."

"Jed Hart," he said, shaking the hand. Corn looked up quickly. "I'm the real Jed Hart, Corn. They didn't kill me at Nineveh. Sheridan wouldn't stand for that." Jed looked evenly at Corn. "I just rode in from Montana, Corn. I didn't kill that rancher. But I'm going to find out who did."

Corn pulled at his beard.

"Figured your last name was Hart. Remember you from being in town, before the war, with your pappy. You filled out some in six years. Knowed you'd tell me your name if you got nothing to hide. But you gonna ride into trouble. Don't count on no help from the town marshal. He does what big brother tells him. And Marshal Partlow uses the Slash S guns to back it up."

Corn sent a stream of black juice squirting toward the fire.

"Sure like to mosey in with you, boy. 'Cept, I got to get back to my works. Your mother lives first house north of the school. If I can help . . ."

Jed grinned. "If I run into any rattlesnakes or coyotes, I'll save them for you, Corn." Jed finished lashing his blanket roll on the saddle and checked the Winchester in the boot. He loosened the six-gun in its leather home and swung up on the horse.

Corn pointed a finger at Jed.

"You ever need help, you ask for me at the Pastime. They sell my corn there. They'll get word to me."

Jed waved and moved the sorrel on the stage road to town.

Memories surged back as he traveled the familiar trail south: the alder grove where he shot his first deer; deep pools at the curves in Sein Creek where he caught trout; the swimming hole they dug half a mile from town. Then he could see the town buildings. He had not passed any lanes leading off the main road that looked like they went into big cattle spreads. He would have to find out where the Slash S was located.

Hendersonville looked about the same. There was the new saloon and the attached hotel, even a few new houses. The Cattleman's Saloon still was the biggest. Very few people on the streets yet. He walked the sorrel through town on Main Street, then circled around to the end of Front Street and rode down the other main avenue. The town was built around the cross of the two dusty streets.

He rode to the schoolhouse, paused a moment looking at the house north of it, then turned and galloped back to Main Street and the Cattleman's Saloon. If there were any activity, it would be there.

By now, a dozen cowboys lounged in the chairs in front of the place. They looked up quickly, then glanced away. They seemed to be waiting for someone. There were only two other horses at the tie rail when Jed looped his reins over the peeled pole. He watched the lineup of men and wondered if someone were hiring new hands. Before he had made up his mind, two horses pounded into town from the west, stopping in a flurry of dust at the rail.

Jed noticed the larger man first. He was at least six feet four, with wide shoulders under a light range jacket and a large head topped by a white Stetson. He wore a full moustache. As he reined in, the big cowboy looked at the wranglers who started moving forward.

"Hold it!" It was a command from the big rider. "You mavericks want to be looked at, just get in line. Mr. Partlow's gonna have a drink, then he'll talk. Now line up and shut up."

The second man had dismounted behind the larger one and marched into the saloon. Partlow, Jed thought. That was the man who owned the Slash S. The big one would be his ramrod. Jed watched as the men formed a ragged line. The last one, a boy not over fifteen, had on range clothes and a six-gun that looked half a hand too large for him. He stood as tall as the others, but his youth was obvious.

The foreman of the Slash S dropped off his horse and walked along the line, sizing up each man. He said nothing until he came to the third one.

"Out, Harry. Out!" He jerked his thumb, motioning away from the line. The puncher with no hat looked at his boots and backed away. "We don't hire no gutless blue bellies. We use just top cowhands who can fight!"

Nervous laughter scattered down the line. The foreman waved out one more man. The third one who got the thumb refused to move.

"I'll let Mr. Partlow say if he wants me or not," the stocky wrangler said.

The foreman grabbed the man's jacket front and pulled him out of line. A vicious backhanded blow toppled the smaller man into the dust of the street. He came to his knees cursing and reached for his six-gun.

"Make a play, cowboy," the Slash S ramrod said. "Go ahead and draw. Nothing'd start out my day better than putting a couple of holes in your worthless carcass."

He waited a few moments; the cowboy's hands relaxed, and he stood up slowly.

"If you ain't gonna draw, get out of town!"

The man turned and, keeping his hands well away from his gun, moved slowly down the street.

When the foreman came to the youth, he broke into a laugh.

The boy's face showed a sudden flush, and his lip quivered.

"What you laughing at me for?" he demanded hotly.

The foreman choked off his laugh and slapped the boy, spinning him half way around. The big man turned and looked at the men left in line. "Anytime the Slash S has to go to the cradle for its hands . . ."

The deadly click of a cocking six-gun strangled the rest of his sentence. He turned slowly toward the sound, his hand poised at his side over the black-handled Colt.

The boy held his six-gun steadily, centered on the foreman's chest. With his face almost blanched white, the youth backed away two steps. The gun never wavered.

"Ben, you been pushing around people in this town long enough. You been killin' men too long. If nobody else got the guts to stand up to you, I will."

"Put that gun away, boy. You trying to get yourself killed?"

"I'm gonna kill you, Matheson. Just like

you killed my pa. You never gave him no chance. You gunned him down for no reason. That was three years ago. Now I'm big enough to settle with you."

"Then let me draw against you. Make it fair, kid!"

The boy laughed. "Fair? You don't know fair! Now you start saying your prayers!" He raised the gun and aimed carefully.

When Jed was sure the boy would shoot, he moved swiftly and slashed his fist down on the gun wrist a second before the hammer dropped. The bullet slammed into the ground at Matheson's feet, and the gun spun to the ground.

Ben stared at the gun for a fraction of a second; then, realizing he was unhurt, he charged the six feet toward the boy. He slashed a right hand into the youth's jaw. It staggered him back, but he caught his balance and came toward Ben, swinging wildly. The bigger man blocked the punches easily, then smashed his right and left hands into the boy's jaw and nose. Ben's fists kept pounding the youth, first into his stomach, then again to his jaw and eye. His last blow caught the boy on the point of the chin and dropped him to the dust.

Ben pulled him up with one hand and

drove another fist into his mouth. The young fighter toppled to his back and rolled over, holding his hands over his head.

"Try and bushwhack me, will you, kid? I don't know who your old man was, but he must have been the same kind of trash you are!"

Ben pulled the boy out of the dirt and drew back to hit him again when a .44 barked at close range. Ben turned.

Jed stood ten feet away, his gun out, a wisp of black powder smoke trailing from the muzzle.

"The little guy's had enough, Ben."

"Enough?" Surprise scudded over the big man's face. "He just about kill *you,* cowboy?"

Jed shook his head.

"Then what call you got telling me he's had enough?" Ben dropped the boy, and he fell into the dust again. Then he stared at Jed. "You the hombre who knocked his gun down, ain't you?"

Jed nodded.

"You put that hog leg away. We'll shake hands."

Jed dropped the .44 back in leather, and Ben came up. He stood looking at Jed for a moment, then slashed out his left fist into

Jed's stomach. Before Jed could react, a right hand bounced off his jaw, staggering him back.

"Get him boys," Ben yelled, and three of the men in the line jumped Jed and held him. Ben moved up, smiling.

"Stranger, time you had a lesson in manners. We don't hold to saddle tramps horning in on our business. I don't take kindly to a man holding a gun on me. What the kid got is just a sample of what's ready for you. Toss his gun away, boys. Don't want him to get no ideas."

His gun was pulled from him, and at the same time a lasso settled over him and cinched tight. Jed knew what was coming and tried to pull off the rope. Before he could, it snapped around his chest, pinning his arms to his sides. All he could do was reach up and grab the taut rope.

Ben Matheson had mounted and caught the rope. He snubbed it around the saddle horn, and before Jed could move, Ben sent his horse pounding down Main Street. Jed was jerked off his feet and towed along like a log, bumping and scraping through the dusty road. He rolled and bounced. It took every ounce of his strength to hold his head away from the ground.

He felt his pants legs burn through, and

he knew the skin was gone. He tried to hold his legs wide to act as skids and keep him upright. But as soon as he did, Ben made a slanting turn, rolling him over and over in the choking dust. At the far end of Main Street, Ben stopped and turned his horse in a tight circle. He looked down at Jed.

"Stranger, don't meddle. Anytime you want to match me, you just call me out. I'll be more than obliged."

Ben spurred his mount forward and Jed suffered another skidding, burning ride down Main Street. He lost his hat, and now his shirt was torn in shreds, his arms raw and bleeding, and his face a mass of welts and bruises. As the horse slowed in front of the saloon, he tried to pull himself up and run, but his strength gave out and he fell, rolling over and over in a hopeless mass of arms and legs and loops of rope.

The ten prospective Slash S riders were silent as Ben stopped. He motioned for two of them to untie Jed. They leaned him against the saloon tie rail.

Jed's head was spinning and fuzzy. He did not know if he could remain standing or not. He wanted to throw up and crawl off somewhere and die. Every square inch of his skin felt on fire. One of his eyes had swelled shut. He stared weakly at the form of Ben Matheson in front of him.

"That was your first ride, saddle bum. Your next one will be out of town feet first up cemetery hill. I catch you in town again, I'll gun you down." He turned to the men in the line. "Inside, you wranglers. Mr. Partlow'll take a look at you."

Jed slumped down on the boardwalk of the saloon, holding his head trying to stop the hammering. He looked up and located the horse trough. Just standing up was an effort. He pulled himself up on the rail and staggered the first few feet, then caught his balance and stumbled to the water.

Kneeling beside the trough, Jed splashed water over his face and arms. It stung like acid. He could see out of only one eye. Jed washed his arms and rolled up the tattered remains of his shirt sleeves.

He needed to rest, to lick his wounds and make some plans. As the shock faded away, a thousand bruises and scrapes and skinned spots started yammering home the pain.

He sat there trying to remember where he left his horse. He saw the sorrel being led toward him by a tall boy. It was the one who had shot at Ben. The boy had Jed's hat and gun, too.

"Mister, I don't know whether to thank you for saving my life or be mad cause you didn't let me kill Ben."

Jed wanted to grin, but he did not. "Know how you feel. What's your name, son?"

"Luke Rath."

A bruise spread under Luke's eye, and his lip was torn, but he looked in better shape than Jed felt.

"Hello, Luke. My name's Jed. Know where a guy could camp for a couple of days to heal up?"

"Sure do! Down by the big bend in the creek. And I'll come into town to get supplies for us. I'll be like your pard."

"Something like that, Luke. Is that big oak tree still there?"

"Yeah. You been here before?"

"Long time ago, Luke."

Jed had seen the woman's skirt swishing across the dusty street, but he was surprised when the high-button shoes and full skirt stopped in front of him. He looked up slowly, and his amazement multiplied into awkwardness. Standing in front of him was the prettiest girl he had ever seen. Her prim, high-necked dress was a practical print, with white ruffles on the long sleeves and at the throat. What he noticed most were the black eyes that seemed to be burning into his bones as he stood slowly. Then he saw the eyes really were not black; they were a dark violet set in an oval face. Light-blonde hair fell to her shoulders.

She was frowning, and it was some time before Jed realized she was not looking at him, but at Luke.

"Luke, you promised me!" she said sternly. "You gave me your word you would attend every day until the end of May."

Luke shuffled his feet and tried to look somewhere else, but his glance came back to her oval face.

"Aw, Miss White. I've been busy. And I've got to look for work."

"We went over that before, Luke. You know how important an education is these days. Why, this town needs a doctor, and a lawyer, and even another minister."

"Ma'am," Jed said.

She turned to him, her frown gone, one of scorn replacing it.

"Ma'am, maybe I could talk to Luke . . ."

She stopped him with a wave of her hand. "With a gun tied that low, I wouldn't trust you to talk to our preacher. If you'll leave this boy alone, he'll turn out fine."

She turned back to Luke. "I'll see you in class at eight thirty, Luke Rath, or I'll go see your mother right after school!"

She turned and marched across the street.

Jed looked at Luke. "You better get ready for school, Luke. The lady said you promised. A man has to live up to his word — every time!"

Luke whacked his hat against the pump. "Aw, gee! I don't see why. What can I learn in just a few weeks? Now's when they're hiring. I need a job."

"You promised."

"Well, O.K. But if you need any help, I'll be around."

Jed watched Luke Rath walk away. It was a long step to the saddle. He was feeling stronger now. He sat the horse and turned her toward Sein Creek. The first thing he had to do was wash about a pound of gravel out of his hide.

Chapter Three

Sein Creek meandered north and swung within a quarter of a mile of town. The headwaters were seven or eight miles away in a little valley not far from where Jed's father had homesteaded on the Double H ranch. He wondered what had happened to it.

Jed swung down off the sorrel and ground-tied her as he looked at the thicket of willow. It was on the far side of the creek and would make a good screen for his camp. He forded the cool water, tied the horse, and took off her saddle.

A few moments later, he had pulled his boots and socks off and stripped off his pants and ripped shirt. The water was cold as he scrubbed, but it felt good against the bruises. He scrubbed himself as best he could, then shaved in cold water.

After washing his jeans, he laid them over a branch to sun-dry and pulled on his last shirt. He stretched out on his blanket and tried to think through his next move. It would be a week before he quit hurting from that dragging he had taken. The water had reduced the swelling around his eye, and he could see almost normally from it.

Jed saw a movement to his right and his six-gun swung up silently. When the creature moved again, he fired. The rabbit spun backward and lay still. Jed cleaned and skinned it, and ten minutes later a thin wisp of smoke drifted skyward. He roasted the rabbit on a spit, turning it slowly until the meat cooked a soot-tinged brown. Using the last bit of salt from his salt sack, Jed seasoned the lunch and tried it. When the rabbit had turned into a pile of picked bones, Jed decided he had eaten worse.

His pants and socks had dried, so he finished dressing and repacked his gear. Home, that was what he had to cover first. He had to see his mother. What could he tell her? What could he say?

He whittled a toothpick and used it. The war had taught him one lesson: Never charge into an area without scouting it and finding out as much as possible about it. His mother had the facts he needed.

But he could not simply ride in and see her. Someone might recognize him. They would think he was the killer. Jed looked at the sun. It was almost noon, but he could not afford to wait until darkness.

Jed thought it through again. Something seemed obvious, but he could not grasp it. His mother was living in the first house north of the schoolhouse on Front Street. He was north and east of town. Of course! He didn't have to go through town. Just ride into the very edge of town to his mother's house and go in the back way.

He pulled on his hat and set it low over his eyes. That and the different shirt would help. He rubbed some mud over the Block B brand on his horse's hip to hide the strange brand. Then he saddled the sorrel, lashed on his gear, and rode out.

He felt better. The minor cuts and scrapes had stopped yammering at him, and now the major bruises and tears let him know where they were. His legs and arms were the worst. In a week, he would be as mean as ever, and he was thankful he had not picked up a .44 slug.

Jed felt like the point man of a patrol going into enemy territory as he moved past the first house where the prairie ended and the town began. His eyes picked up every detail — the house, the dirt street, a carriage — and he automatically sifted and evaluated it. Everything looked peaceful. He was being overcautious. If he acted naturally, no one would pay any attention to him.

Jed passed one more house without being noticed and walked his horse to the side fence of the little house. He tied the animal and walked to the back door. His first knock brought no response. He knocked again — harder.

The door opened slowly, and a woman's face peered around it.

"Yes?"

"Ma?"

The door came open more, a surprised, unbelieving expression flooding the woman's face.

"Jed?"

The door swung wide, and she reached for him.

"Oh, Jed, I can hardly believe my eyes." Tears came and washed down her cheeks. She pulled him inside and stared at him.

"What happened? You're all scratched and hurt. You hurt bad, Jed?"

"No, Ma. Just scratched up some. I been gone a long time, Ma. They didn't kill me at Nineveh, and no matter what you heard, I didn't kill that rancher. I'm here to find out who did."

"Ah knowed they never killed you at Nineveh, Jed. I just knowed it down in my bones!"

Mrs. Hart was a large woman, nearly five feet nine, big-boned and equal to the rough frontier life. Her hair was gray now and in a bun at the back of her head. She let the tears come as she held him close.

Jed hardly recognized her. She looked sixty, not in her forties. She had lost weight; her hands had turned soft and her eyes were sunken and dull.

"You're looking fine, Ma." He paused and she smiled. "Ma, I didn't know they told you I was dead. After the war, I just moved around a lot, didn't want nobody telling me what to do for a while. But I'm glad to be home."

She closed the door and led him through the kitchen into the small dining room.

"Ain't much," she said motioning to the room.

"It's fine, Ma. Just fine."

"No it ain't. Your Pa and me had that ranch house out to the Double H, and now it's gone, and Pa's gone, too." She looked up at him, tears welling in her eyes.

"You don't know 'bout Pa, do you?"

Jed shook his head.

"Your Pa was out with the stock, trying

to calm them down in a storm. Ridin' round trying to settle them down when lightning struck a tree behind the herd. The cattle spooked. Almost three-hundred head came right over him." She was crying now. Jed put a hand on her shoulder, and she reached for it. She held it tightly.

"It's good to have you home, Jed." He patted her shoulder.

"Crying? Crying is for going away, Ma. Not for coming home." He looked around the room and remembered some of the furniture. There were a hundred questions he wanted to ask, but this was not the time. One point had to be settled, though.

"Ma, can you tell me about the ranch? Did you lose it after Pa died?"

The woman dried her pale-blue eyes that were so much like her son's and looked at him evenly.

"Yes, I lost it, Jed. After your Pa was killed, I sort of went to pieces. The Slash S had been trying to buy us out for a year. But Pa wouldn't sell. Then, when he died, they came 'round the very next day and told me they'd take over for me and all. Said I should sign a lease agreement, and first thing I knowed, they said I sold the place and the cattle for three hundred dollars and this little house."

"Everett Partlow?"

"Yes, him. The preacher said it wasn't right and went to the sheriff at the county seat, but nothin' ever happened. The marshal here in town is Partlow's kin. It happened over two years ago now."

"I'll fix it, Ma. I'll put everything right back where it ought to be!"

"Cain't fight the Partlows. They own the law. They hire best guns. Cain't fight the Partlows."

"I can, Ma. And I aim to."

They went on talking, catching up on six years of news of the town and family. The afternoon crept past, and before Jed knew it, the shadows had lengthened.

There was a noise at the front door, and Jed jumped up, his hand ready by his gun.

The door opened, and a girl came in. When she turned, Jed saw it was the schoolteacher.

"Hello, Mrs. Hart," she said, and paused. "Oh, I didn't know you had company." She turned to go into the other room, but Jed's mother stopped her.

"Emily, come here."

The young woman came forward, watching Jed. When she was sure who it was, she stopped, her arms planted on hips.

"It is you. Why can't you leave decent

38

folks alone?" Her face had flushed with anger.

Mrs. Hart looked at the girl, a question on her face.

"I don't understand, Emily. You met Jed before?"

"Fact is we met," Jed said. "Down at the watering trough this morning."

"That's right, and I certainly don't . . ." She stopped, looked from one to the other, and then laughed softly. "Then you must be Jed Hart, Mrs. Hart's long lost son." She looked at Jed again. "And you're the one they say killed Mr. Vanderzanden. You have your nerve, Jed Hart, coming here and dragging your mother into all this!"

"Just a minute, fancy-talking lady!"

Before Jed could continue, his mother stepped between them.

"Children! children! There's no need to shout. Why don't we talk this over during supper. I've got some stew that's almost done."

Emily White nodded and went into the far bedroom. When she came back, she had combed her hair out. She did not look at Jed. Instead, she set the table for two; then, with a shrug, she added a third plate.

Jed and his mother kept reminiscing and laughing, but Miss White sat still, saying very little. A small red spot of resentment still burned in her right cheek. As soon as the meal was over, they rose.

"I have some work to do for school. Please excuse me, Mrs. Hart." She looked at Jed. "As for you, Mr. Hart, it's amazing such a saintly, God-fearing woman like Mrs. Hart could have a son such as you!" She turned and strode into the other room.

Jed laughed at her and soothed his mother's feelings.

"Emily White usually isn't that way, Jed. She's a kind, pleasant, and smart woman. Went to two years of teacher-training school back East. Her board and room money is what keeps us both eating."

Jed nodded and looked out the window. It was dark now. He asked his mother directions to the Slash S ranch.

"That's the old Porter place, just six miles across the fields from the Double H," she said.

"I'm going to make a call on your friend Mr. Partlow. I'll offer him a chance to give us back our ranch peaceable." He paused and smiled at his mother. "Course, I don't really expect him to."

Chapter Four

Jed came through the grove of oak in back of Partlow's Slash S and tied his horse to a branch. He took off his spurs and everything that might rattle out of his pockets and put it in the saddlebag. Jed checked his six-gun — five loads in the cylinder and the hammer on an empty chamber.

He moved silently over the crest of the hill and paused at the edge of the grove to look over the spread. Partlow had expanded it since Porter owned it. Two new barns, a big stack of leftover hay and a blacksmith shed. There were two lights in the ranch house and Jed moved toward them.

He felt as if he were back in Tennessee again, moving in short bursts, then waiting, crawling along on his elbows and toes through an open space, blending with whatever cover there was. His senses were alert, ready for anything he heard that was not normal. He went past the corral. A door banged, and Jed stopped, pressing himself against a post of the corral. He saw no movement. The moon sent a half-light over the ranch yard. Jed moved again. He had not asked about a dog. Every ranch had a dog. But Jed saw none. Maybe Ev Partlow was too mean to keep a dog. He swung wide around the bunkhouse, which was fronted by the kitchen, and reached the side wall of the house. It was made of oak logs and sod and had lots of chinks.

Jed worked his way along to the window that was lighted. He took off his hat and edged up to the very corner of the window where he could see into the room.

It was set up like an office, with a small desk, a chair, and a bookshelf. Jed could see two men, Partlow and Ben Matheson. There was a door on the far side of the room. Jed moved to the door quietly, watching the yard for a stray hand who might give him away. But there was no one. He drew his gun and in one quick motion unlatched the door, pushed it open, and stepped inside.

"Hold it right where you are!" Jed's voice was sharp, and Ben Matheson settled back in his chair. "Keep your hands up where I can see them or you're a dead man."

He reached behind him and pushed the door closed.

"Who is this," Partlow asked.

"Some saddle tramp I gave a drag ride this morning," Ben said. " 'Pears he didn't like it none too well."

"Quiet! Stand up, both of you." They did, and both wore gun belts. "Loosen your gunbelts and let them drop. Now!" They did, Ben's hands fumbling from anger.

"Partlow, take out your purse and toss it over here — quickly!" The man took his time pulling the long leather purse with the snap top out of his coat pocket, then threw it; Jed caught it and rammed it into his pants pocket.

"Partlow, I don't want to forget you. You and me are going to see a lot of each other."

Partlow shrugged, trying to show his contempt. "The only time I'll see you again is when the marshal hangs you."

Partlow stood about five feet ten, thin as an oak sapling. His face was pinched, and he wore a business suit of gray broadcloth and a fancy shirt, white cuffs showing at his wrists.

"You don't know who I am, do you, Partlow?"

"And I don't care."

"You talk too fancy to be a Kansan. You must be a carpetbagger come out here to skin us natives."

Ben had been edging around closer to Jed. Jed had been ignoring him, leading him on. Now Ben made his lunge, and Jed was ready. He sidestepped quickly and brought his six-gun down viciously on the side of the big man's head. Ben fell heavily to the dirt floor and rolled over groaning.

Jed went on talking to Partlow as if nothing happened.

"You skinned one too many natives, Partlow. My name is Hart, Jed Hart."

Partlow looked up quickly, surprise shading his face, then vanishing.

"You cheated my widowed mother out of her ranch, and you did it all legal. But I don't go along with that kind of legal. It's too slow, anyway. I could settle it right now with a forty-four slug in your belly and watch you die slow."

Partlow wiped one white hand across his pale forehead.

"But I'm not 'bout to do that, Partlow. That would be too easy on you."

The thin man relaxed a little, and his old bravado came back.

"Hart, you're bluffing. I know a bluffer

when I see one. Sure, I got your mother's ranch away at a minimum cost. That's business. In Philadelphia, it's done all the time. Just try to get any legal decisions about it. I'll laugh you out of court. I was a lawyer for a while, you know."

Jed's hand tensed on the iron. He was very close to shooting the man. He took a quick gulp of air and quieted his racing thoughts.

"Partlow, let me tell you something! I know your kind. I've seen a lot, and I've killed my share. You'll probably be the next one. Let me tell you what I'm going to do. I'll take back the Double H ranch you stole. I'm gonna take back seven hundred and fifty head of prime beef you stole. If you or your hired gunmen try to stop me, they'll wind up face down in the dirt."

He patted the purse in his pocket. "We'll call whatever is in here a payment on interest for the past two years." Jed looked down at Ben, who still sat on the floor holding his head.

"Partlow, tell your fat friend here the next time we meet, he won't get off so lucky." Jed backed up two steps to the door, opened it with a hand behind his back, and stepped out into the cool evening air. He checked the deserted ranch yard before running hard for the corral. Jed expected to hear shots from the doorway, but there were none. He sprinted past the corral and up the slope to the edge of the oak grove. No one chased him. He trotted over the rise and swung up on his horse. Still there was no alarm from below. Jed smiled. Ev Partlow knew his men would not have a chance of catching him. He would accept this setback as a minor business inconvenience. Ben Matheson would be another matter. He had been humiliated before his boss. Ben would be out for a showdown as soon as he could, and at almost any cost. It would be a pleasure when it came, Jed thought, as he moved his mount out at a gallop.

As soon as the door closed behind Jed Hart, the thin man sat back at his desk.

"You can get up now Ben. The nasty man has gone." There was an edge of sarcasm in his voice that satisfied Ev Partlow. He had no love for big men like Ben, and it was good to see one in the dirt. Ben stood up and swayed against the desk.

"Sit down, Ben, before you knock over my desk. No, we're not going to chase him. Unless you can trail a man at night!" He watched the big man slump into a chair and wince at the pain in his head.

46

"We simply have a new element to consider in our venture, Ben. What we thought would be an easy mark has turned out to be more complicated. The reports said the son had been killed in the war. Who could expect him to return from the dead?"

Everett Partlow made a tepee out of his fingers and tapped his thumbs together. He was thinking. In the bank in Philadelphia, they had called him a banker's banker. Very little got past him when he was working. Then there was that unfortunate shortage of funds that no one — certainly not he — could explain. While there was no legal action taken, the president thought it would be better if Ev moved to another state. Ev did, and the missing funds somehow found their way along with him. It had all been so childishly simple.

But right now Ev was more interested in thinking around his current problem. The young man was certainly determined. And he seemed proficient. He had the courage to confront his enemy and tell him what would happen.

Jed Hart would have to be eliminated. A quiet funeral — with Ben officiating — would be best. Ev knew Ben would be glad to do the whole job, from the first trigger pressure right through to the final spade of dirt.

But what if Ben could not find Jed? Time was what he needed now. He had to maintain his lily-white posture at least for another week. It could take Ben longer than that to track down Jed. In that time, Jed could raise all sorts of problems.

The "Wanted" poster was safest. He looked at Ben. He still needed the big man. Ev Partlow reached in the desk drawer and brought out a bottle. He passed it to Ben, who uncapped it and without a word tipped it skyward, letting the green whiskey sear down his throat. He lowered it and handed it back.

"Thanks, Mr. Partlow. I'm feeling better."

"Go get Ira. Have him get ready to ride."

"Tonight, Mr. Partlow?"

Ev looked at Ben, and the corners of his mouth twitched and drew down in a frown. Ben hurried outside, his bruised head forgotten.

The plan forming in Ev Partlow's mind now blossomed. Jed Hart was wanted in connection with the Vanderzanden killing. That was well known. It was time the marshal put out a "Wanted" bulletin on him. And since he had now also robbed one of the most respected ranchmen of the valley, it would be a dead-or-alive reward poster. Ev tapped his fingers together, staring straight ahead but seeing nothing.

A reward of three hundred dollars should be enough. That would get at least twenty men off their haunches and out bounty-hunting by noon. He smiled. And they said in Philadelphia that he could not cope with the wild, wild West. Cope? He was making the West dance to his tune. And how it was dancing! Money made it dance. Money made the whole town sit up and respect Everett Partlow.

He took out a piece of paper and a stub of a pencil and wrote out the poster. He had done it before and knew the vital elements. This time he included what the killer was last seen wearing and the brand of the sorrel horse he rode. Ben could fill that in when he came back.

Ev thought about the threat to the old Double H ranch. Was his line camp there in any real danger? Ev found it hard to believe that one man, even a rash one like Jed, would move in and try to take over a line camp by himself. Did he have any help, anyone in town who was on his side? That was one problem he would have to clear up. Ev thought it through and was certain Jed would not hurt his line camp. That left only Jed himself to deal with.

Ev took out a much-folded letter and read it again. Every time he looked at it, the formal script sent a thrill of anticipation through him.

"Dear Everett. At this time I am not certain if I shall run or not. A great deal depends on my business at home. I hope to serve the state again in Washington, but if I am not able to for any reason, I would consider it an honor to suggest your name to the State Committee. I feel sure that with my endorsement you will have a very easy time in getting the nomination. And in Kansas to be nominated by the Republicans is almost the same as being elected.
"Your most dedicated servant,
Samuel C. Pomeroy."

Ev Partlow smiled at the paper. The dear senator did not know it, but whether he wanted to run or not, he would not be taking office again. There were too many forces at work to deny him the nomination. And even if the incumbent were nominated, there were many dangerous territories he would be campaigning in. Accidents had been known to happen to politicians in the wilds of Kansas.

Five minutes later, Ira came in ready to ride. Ben told Ev the brand, the Block B, and the wanted poster was ready. Ev gave the sealed envelope to Ira.

"You took a poster like this in to town once before. I want you to do the same thing. Find the marshal, wherever he is. Tell him to get this poster printed tonight. It has to be printed and posted before sunup. Now say that back to me."

Partlow waited while the rider repeated the instructions.

"Now get out of here and ride hard!"

The hand hurried out, and Partlow turned to Ben. He backhanded the larger man a slashing blow across the cheek.

"I want some guards around this place, Ben. If you can't keep the ranch safe, I'll have to get somebody who will!"

"Yes, sir. Yes, Mr. Partlow." Ben turned and went back toward the bunkhouse.

Ev watched him go and thought about the letter again. Just one week! He had to hold on for a week without a scandal blowing up and he would have that nomination. After that, anything that happened could be played down as "politically motivated" and all those high-sounding phrases.

The prize was almost in his grasp. When he got to Washington, he would turn Kansas into his own private club, and he would hold the only key to the gate. It all depended on the next week.

Behind him, a door opened into the main part of the ranch house.

"Ev, it's getting late."

He turned and frowned. Then as his eyes sought out the soft lines of her young body that showed against the cotton nightgown, his frown faded. "I'll be right up, dear." She turned, and the gown drew taut around her full body.

He sighed. He would have to do something about Minnie, too. The minute he got the nomination the Democrats would be looking for everything they could find to use against him. And while Minnie was one of his true joys, she would have to go back to Wichita, at least until after the election.

Ev Partlow snorted. Why did he have to give her up? Then he remembered the imprinted stationery, the expensive feel of it, the title, and he smiled again. It was worth it. In Washington, there would be lots of women. Lots of women who would be anxious to please the junior U.S. senator from the great state of Kansas!

Chapter Five

Jed Hart looked back at the ranch house before he set the sorrel on a steady trot toward town. He came to a familiar fork in the road and looked north. The Double H ranch was up there. In a half hour, he could be there.

He let the sorrel blow, listening for hoof beats behind him. Jed wondered what the old home place looked like.

He had told Ev Partlow he was going to take it, he could do that right now!

Jed pulled the horse's head around and rode down the new trail. It climbed a small hill, then angled sharply through a narrow valley and up a gradual slope that would bring him into the ranch from the side. He let the horse drink at Merry Brook, then walked her on toward the faint outline of the barn two hundred yards away. The barn was dark, but there was a glow of a kerosene lamp in the kitchen of the ranch house. Jed looked up at the stars. It was nearly midnight. He tied his horse to a scattering of hickory brush behind the barn and stepped warily in the open door of the unpainted building. He found two horses in stalls, unsaddled. Why were they inside instead of in the corral? Two mounts meant two wranglers in the house. There was no other livestock in the barn or surrounding pens. The Slash S must use the place only as a line camp when they had cattle pastured here.

Jed slid out of the shadow of the barn and ran quickly to the tool shed. There had been a bunk in the end of it. He checked, but it was empty. Now he approached the lighted window, Jed took his hat off and edged up to look inside. The lamp sat on the roughhewn table he and his father had worked so hard on. It was littered with trash, cigarette burns, and dust.

One end had been cleaned off, and two men sat playing cards. He saw stacks of copper coins, but no guns. Slipping away from the window, Jed ran back to the barn. He took both horses out of the building and whacked them hard on the rumps. They would not stop running until they were halfway back to their home corral at the Slash S. He took his own horse behind the house and tied her.

Back at the door of the ranch house, he lifted the latch slowly, then kicked the door open and jumped into the room. His six-gun was cocked and ready.

"Don't move!" Jed commanded. "Keep your hands on top of the table." He moved closer to them. They had been playing poker with stacks of Indian-head pennies as chips.

"High stakes game?"

One of the men laughed. "It's what we can afford on twenty dollars a month." He frowned. "You aimin' to rob us?"

Jed laughed. He saw they carried no guns. "I'm just running you off my ranch. This is private property."

"This is Partlow land, the Slash S," the heavier man said.

Jed turned the muzzle of his .44 at him.

"My friend says this is private land, and you two have five minutes to pick up what's yours and gallop out of here. I'll keep your guns, so you don't get unhealthy ideas."

They laid out their six-guns and one rifle, and each rolled up a blanket and an extra pair of pants and went to the door.

"Your horses are already halfway home. I

don't want you guys to come back too soon. You should be able to get to the Slash S by daylight. It's only six miles."

"Six miles?" one of the riders said. "I ain't walked six miles since my roan broke her leg ten years back."

"Right now you walk or dance over lead."

He nodded, shouldered the thin blanket roll, and headed for the trail. Jed knew how most cowboys hated to walk. It was beneath their station; they were riding men. And it hurt their feet. Both would be footsore and mad as plucked prairie chickens by the time they hit the Slash S.

Jed watched them fade into the darkness. He sat on the steps and waited. He had developed a strong patience in the army.

When he was sure the men were not coming back, he went into the house and looked around. It was of frame construction — rough lumber on the outside with one coat of paint that had been wind-blasted off years ago. His pa had never got around to finishing the inside walls. The two-by-four studs marched around the room.

Jed picked up the lamp and took it into the next room, which had been the dining and living room. It was cleaner than the kitchen, but two years of dust covered everything. Half of the furniture was still there, and he could see small animal tracks through the dust. He went on into his room. It was almost intact. The bed still had quilts on it, and he found mementos of his youth still tacked to the rough walls: an Indian headband and the two broken arrows they had pulled out of a man on a wagon after an Indian attack. The faded certificate of his eighth-grade graduation. That had been his father's biggest joy.

Jed turned abruptly and went back to the kitchen and through it into a small woodshed. After his father had fought the snow drifts all that first winter for firewood, he had built a woodshed to store the winter's fuel. Then he had another idea.

Jed toed the chips and dirt away from the center of the woodshed. It had been used most by birds lately. His toe struck what he was looking for. He took a piece of wood and shoved the chips and dirt away until he had exposed wooden planking in a three-foot square. Jed found the iron ring in the side of the plank and pulled. Nothing happened. He got a long stick and pried up on the planks. At last, they broke free. The planks rose now as he pulled the ring of the trap door.

Jed held the lamp low and looked down. Then he moved down a few steps. It was a tunnel that had been braced and shored like a mine drift. The tunnel was dry and solid. It would last one hundred years, or until the timbers rotted. Jed did not follow it farther.

His father had been a coal miner in the East. When he decided to come West and begin raising cattle, he never quite lost his love for mining. In the winters, when snow blotted out everything on the Kansas plains, he would take his shovel and pick and move underground. At first, it was just a hobby. Then he decided it was an escape route in case of an Indian attack. It went underground almost fifteen feet, then slanted up to the splash of willows below the barn. It was over three hundred feet long and four to five feet high.

Jed thought of all the work that went into it, but he realized the satisfaction his father must have felt. He dropped the cover back over the tunnel and kicked the dirt and chips back in place.

Outside, he looked over the little spread. The water from Merry Brook was sure and steady all summer. It came from springs in the high ground behind the house. They had plenty of water for seven hundred head, maybe more. He could dam up that low place just below the corral to catch some of the spring run-off.

The corral was the only big change. The Slash S men had enlarged it and put a smaller corral to one side. He stood there hands on his hips, looking over the moonlit yard.

Six years ago, he had not been interested in cattle or horses. His one big thought had been to get into the army. And he had done that. But war was not what he had thought it would be. He had seen enough shooting and killing. He knew he might have to kill again, but this time it would be for his own piece of land, his own ranch!

As he walked to the house, his army training came back. Just because he took off the uniform, he could not forget the logic of an attack or how to outthink the enemy. Only now the enemy was different. It had been bad strategy to come here tonight. It was done in haste and without plan. He knew he could not hold the Double H. Why else had he sent the horses running home first and made the men walk?

It had been an emotional decision, and it could have been costly. As soon as the horses came home, someone on the Slash S would recognize them and know where they came from. He moved quickly into the house and gathered up the hand guns and put then in a flour sack. After one last look around, Jed blew out the lamp and went out and closed the door. He braced a stick against it and hurried up to his horse.

Jed had made a raid deep into enemy territory, and with the first streaks of dawn, the Partlows would be out with half their guns looking for him — to gun him down.

With a shout, he put the horse into motion. He had to get back to town or to a well-traveled road before daylight so his tracks could mix with other riders.

On his way, he laid a trail that would give fits to the best Indian trackers. He backtracked, circled, and recrossed the same area three or four times. When he hit Sein Creek, he rode in the hock-deep water for two miles before he came out on the road and made time into town.

There would be enough traffic on the road to blot out his prints before the Slash S riders could get that far. He saw the town in front of him and looked at the stars. They were fading fast. He did not realize he had used up so much time laying the trail. Now he could go to his mother's house and tell her the old place looked fine, and they would be back working it before she could say "schoolteacher" three times!

He had just passed the first house on North Front Street when he saw the poster. It was tacked to an oak tree that had been used for twenty years as a bulletin board. The poster had not been there the day before. Jed walked his mount up close to read it.

"Wanted: *Dead or Alive.* Jed Hart. $300 reward. This man wanted for the murder of Harold Vanderzanden, local rancher. Born and raised here, Hart was not killed in the war as first believed. This was a ruse to cover up his life of crime, robbery, and murder. When last seen . . ."

Jed did not have to read the rest. Now they had made it official. Anyone recognizing him could gut-shoot him or shoot him in the back without warning — and wind up with three hundred dollars for his trouble. That was more money than a cowhand could make in a year and a half! There would be twenty or thirty gun sharps, loafers, and bar bums gunning for him before the noon lunch bell rang.

Jed sat in the saddle staring at the poster for a moment. He could see his mother's house. But he could not go there now. He felt the crawling sensation on the back of his neck that always meant danger. He rode on evenly, with no obvious haste, but his mind was spinning. He had been shut out of town, and soon men would fan out combing every creek bed, every campsite in the county.

"Corn McIntosh!" Jed said to himself. He thought about what the little man had said. Come to the Pastime. Where was it? Out on West Main Street, almost out of town. In the few hours he had known Corn, he had felt a strong attachment to him. He was sure Corn would help him.

Jed jerked the reins around and sent the sorrel through the prairie and in back of the houses on a short-cut trip to the Pastime. It was still early. He could make inquiries at the Pastime, and if nothing happened, he would see his mother and then ride out of the state until this cooled down. Right now it all depended on the little man who made corn whiskey.

Chapter Six

Jed rode quickly to the Pastime. He continued to the back and tied his horse to a stub fence. The Pastime was the end of the road for serious drinkers in Hendersonville. It perched alone, the last outpost of the town west. Its architecture looked as suspect as the drinkers. The building had been thrown up one afternoon thirty years ago by a man and his two half-wit sons. The front of it was clapboard and had been painted once, but the paint had long since peeled off and the boards themselves were warped and loose in spots where the square-cut nails had rusted away.

A small sign over the door was hand-lettered, but painted with a two-inch paint brush in the crudest way. The door was gone, and a gunny sack split open lengthwise and skewered to another one with two nails served to keep out some of the dust of the street. There were no windows.

Jed pushed back the dirty burlap and ducked inside. It was dark, with one spot of light where a lamp sat on the bar. The bar was a convenience, not a work of art. It was made of two fifty-gallon wooden kegs with two-inch planks nailed to the top. So far, no one had ever broken it. The floor was sand and sawdust evenly mixed. It saved considerable work when a drunk spilled his beer. Jed looked around to see who was drinking this time of day. Only two other customers were there. One had passed out in a chair near the corner and was snoring peacefully. The second man was slumped in a chair, staring into an empty beer mug.

Four or five tables scattered around the room, and it all smelled of stale cigarette smoke, old beer, and cheap corn whiskey. Somewhere there was a different odor; then Jed recognized it — bacon and eggs. It drifted in from the door behind the bar.

Behind the far end of the bar sat a shriveled old man who must have been a hard-drinking seventy. His teeth and hair were gone, but his green eyes were sharp and alert. He had noticed Jed's every move since he came in.

Jed walked directly toward him. No one else in the room was interested in what he had to say. If anyone could help him, it was this grandfather.

"Can you put me in touch with Corn McIntosh? I need to see him right away!"

The green eyes peered at Jed intently for a moment, then with hardly a motion a derringer hovered an inch from Jed's nose.

"Jed Hart, I bet a ninny! Wanted posters all over town on you."

Jed cursed his stupidity. He should have known better than to take the word of a liquored-up old man he met once. It was too late to draw. He would be spitting out brains before his hand touched leather.

To his amazement, the derringer vanished. The old face nodded. "Figured you'd be along." He took another look at Jed. "Come on back. Get you some new clothes and a different horse. That Block B is like a flag waving your name."

Jed followed the old man through the door in back of the bar into a combination kitchen, storeroom, and bedroom. On a bench lay a stack of clothes.

"Put 'em on. Should fit. Keep yer hat. I ain't got nothing in yer size."

Jed stripped off his clothes and pulled on the dark-blue pants and denim shirt. They fit. He buckled on his gun belt and tied down the end of the holster around his leg.

When he looked up, the old man motioned him to a table. It held a plate of bacon and scrambled eggs, a chunk of bread, and a steaming cup of coffee.

Jed felt the weariness creep down into his eyes as he looked at the food. It would help.

"How long since you slept, boy?"

"Too long," Jed said and slid onto the stool.

"Drink the coffee first, all of it! Don't want you going to sleep in the saddle."

Jed drank. It was black and hot and seared his throat, but he felt the effects immediately. His appetite came alive, and he looked at the plate.

The old man watched Jed eat.

"Hungry. That tags you, boy. You got a hungry look in your eye, and that hog's leg is a hungry gun. Shore hope we can fill you up." He paused and rolled a thin smoke from a Bull Durham bag and some brown paper.

"Understand you're new in town, least-wise this time, Jed. Don't take this wanted poster as a bluff. Been done seven times since Marshal Partlow took over. Seven times they hauled in the man dead as a bloated steer. Riders of the Slash S collected the reward money and went on a three-day drunk. Corn said not to let it happen to you."

It was a long speech for the old man. He grinned, his blackened stumps showing decay and a few teeth that had broken.

"You talked to Corn this morning?"

"Nope."

"Then how'd you know what he wants?"

"We got ways of knowing." He spooned more eggs onto the plate and looked at Jed.

"Ease out of town north, same way you come in," he grinned. "You sure played Old Ned with them trackers. They never did find where you came into the Sein. Two of them hit town about five minutes ago. Came straight here, I reckon to watch for you."

Jed held a forkful of eggs on the way to his mouth. "How do you know all this?"

"Got ways. You should be moving."

Jed had no trouble getting out of town. The gray was a big one, with broad shoulders and a full, rounded chest. He had a lot of depth for long riding. Jed walked the horse up the street until he was far enough away from the Pastime, then turned north and rode hard for the first mile. Jed thought over the instructions the old man had given him. As soon as he began describing it, Jed recognized the place. It was Trout Lake, and evidently it was Corn McIntosh's still and hideout. It was a pocket, a small valley back in the hills east of the Double H. It had the lake and a little good land around it, but the hills were covered with oak and hickory. There was not enough good grazing land to make it attractive to a rancher. Jed had fished there when he was a boy.

As he angled away from town, Jed opened the horse and let him run again, then eased him down and held to an easy lope that would burn up the miles. He moved northeast and soon cut the main trail to Medicine Lodge, the county seat some twenty miles cross country. He followed the trail as far as he could, then found the little stream that he knew would empty from the lake. Jed let the horse drink. He washed his face in the stream and winced as the cold water sloshed against the cuts on his face. For a few hours, he had forgotten about the drag ride. Now the soreness crashed down on him as he tried to fight it off. He sat against a tree for a few minutes, battling with the weary fog that had hit him. He washed his face again in the cold water and climbed back in his saddle. He was about halfway there.

The sun had climbed to nine o'clock in the sky as Jed moved his mount up the narrowing path beside the creek, then swung his mount into the stream. He rode in the creek for twenty yards as the narrow walls of the canyon slanted down almost into the water. Suddenly, the valley opened in front of him.

It was larger than Jed remembered. Maybe a half-mile long, but not more than four hundred yards wide. The lake covered over half of the ground, and Jed could see the rows and rows of young corn stretching their stalks skyward. Corn took no chances; he even grew his own raw materials.

A rifle shot slapped into the dirt of the trail ahead of him, and Jed held both hands high. It was the signal and countersign. For just a moment, Jed felt he was back in the army. He held his hands up as he urged the horse forward. Now he could see the cabin. It was small and looked like one room. It had been carefully made from straight oak logs and expertly notched and fitted.

Jed edged the lake and then dropped his hands and galloped the last few yards to the cabin. Corn McIntosh sat on the front step, waiting.

"You didn't waste no time, boy."

Jed swung down and dropped the reins.

"I wasted the last three years. Time I got busy."

"You sure got into trouble fast."

"Some say."

Corn pulled the cob out of the jug at his side and passed it to Jed.

" 'Pears I got a little more book-larning for you. What you know about Everett Partlow?"

Jed frowned. "Some Eastern dude with money who bought a ranch."

Corn nodded. "He's that. He's also one of the smartest men in the county, maybe the whole state. Made a fortune in coal mines back East, he says. Got tired of it, went into banking. Then moved out here after a squabble. He's sharp, he's smart, and he's tough. Far as I know, he's had seven men killed, all legal and proper."

"Let's not make it eight."

"We're aimin' to stop him this time." Corn took another pull from the jug. "But Ev Partlow got bigger fish than you or me. He's a state senator now. Goes up to the capital and talks loud and long. And this year the U.S. Senate seat is up for election.

Old Ev wants the nomination. He's no fit man to represent anybody!"

Jed was surprised by the anger in Corn's voice.

When Corn looked up, some of the ire had drained from his eyes, and he grinned. "That's my problem. I've got to convince Sam Pomeroy to run again. Your problem is staying alive. So far we're doing fine."

"I intend to stay alive. Looks like my next job is to find out who killed Varderzanden."

Corn brushed back his white hair and pulled at his beard.

"Sounds reasonable. Any ideas?"

"Some."

Jed squatted in the dust and began to draw a map. He put in Sein Creek, the Salt Fork of the Arkansas, then the ranches.

"Corn, where did this Vanderzanden live?"

Corn made an X on the map south of the Salt Fork, some eight miles from Hendersonville and fifteen miles from the Slash S.

"Way down there?"

"Yep."

"What would they be doing down there?"

"Who?"

Jed looked at the map again, and when he spoke, he was thinking out loud.

"From what I've seen, Partlow is horse-hiding everyone out of the Sein valley. I saw two deserted ranches up there, and he moved in on Ma and our Double H spread. So I thought Partlow was involved in this ruckus with Vanderzanden, too."

"Could be."

"But it doesn't make sense. Vanderzanden's ranch isn't anywhere near the other ranchers who got cheated out of their land."

Corn nodded and scratched his beard. "Bothered me just a speck, too. Specially when I met you." He paused. "Let me give you something else to think about. Kansas came into the Union in 1861 under the Kansas-Nebraska act, and for the most part we vote Republican — senators, governors, state legislature. We don't like gun-toting Easterners coming out here and shooting up things."

Jed had heard Corn, but his mind had been on other things. His first stop had to be at the Vanderzanden ranch for a talk with the widow. Maybe she could tell him where the shooting took place. He told Corn.

"You'd never make it past town, Jed. You

ain't slept a wink since you woke up yesterday morning at Buckets Crossing. You put six hours of shut-eye in the tank, then I'll tell you how to find the widow lady."

Jed felt waves of fatigue spin through him. He was tired. He would have to sleep soon. Why not now? It would take him two hours of hard riding to get to the Vanderzanden ranch. He looked at the sky; it was about ten in the morning. If he could sleep until four, he could get to the ranch and talk and maybe see the ambush spot before dark. Corn agreed to the plan.

"I'll wake you at three thirty; then you can eat and strike out."

The sleep refreshed Jed. He ate the beans and venison Corn had ready for him and saddled a fresh horse. Jed followed the old-timer's advice, skirting the east side of Hendersonville and cutting cross-country toward the "V" notch in the distant hills where the Salt Fork cut through.

He crossed the stage road going into Hendersonville right on schedule and wasted ten minutes finding the right valley to head up to get on the trail to Vanderzanden's

There was no one in sight when he rode in. The house had a new coat of paint, and

73

the fenced yard bloomed with hollyhocks, petunias, and daisies. The whole yard was an explosion of color on the drab prairie.

A dog barked and rushed at him, but was snubbed by a rope around its collar.

"Prince, down. Stay!" It was a woman's voice, and the dog sat down, but bared his teeth. Jed was in no rush to go past. He waited, and the woman came around the corner of the house, a shotgun in her hands. The way she carried it, Jed knew she had shot it a great many times.

"Evening, ma'am. Corn McIntosh sent me to talk to you. Said you might be able to help." Jed purposely did not use his name — not while she held the shotgun.

She was not over five feet two, and her shoulders seemed too frail for the harsh realities of frontier life. She pushed a strand of dark hair back from her brown eyes.

She smiled, and Jed was surprised. It was a slight, almost girlish face, but sparkled with such a warmth and vigor that the beauty was almost lost.

She lowered the shotgun.

"Lie down, Prince!" She said it commandingly, and the big German shepherd hunkered down, its eyes still not friendly.

"I'm sorry, forgetting my manners. Step down and come inside for some cold lemonade."

Jed swung down and wrapped the reins around the corner of the white fence. He walked self-consciously toward the rear of the house. He felt dirty; he had not shaved, and his clothes were hand-me-downs.

She held the door for him, and he entered the kitchen. The outside of the house looked like Wichita or Kansas City. The inside — handsomely furnished, carefully painted, varnished and waxed until it looked like a showplace — matched.

He sat down after she did and held the cool drink in his hand. He had no idea how she made it so cold. Jed smiled at her.

"I can see this is hard for you. I'm Mrs. Vanderzanden, and it was my husband who was killed three weeks ago. Mr. McIntosh said he would help me in every way he could to track down the men."

"I'm grateful to you, Mrs. Vanderzanden, for your kindness. I want to find the killer, too. My name is Jed Hart."

He watched her mouth tighten.

"I didn't kill your husband. But I want to find out who did so I can clear my name."

"I see. If Mr. McIntosh sent you, that's

enough for me." One of her hands went to her temples, and she held it there a moment as she watched him. "Did you go to school here many years ago?"

He nodded.

"There was a Hart boy two years ahead of me. Could that have been you?"

Jed looked at her again. It had been a long time. He couldn't be sure he remembered her. There had been only twenty kids in the whole school.

"I finished school in 1857," he said.

"I graduated in 1859. It must have been you. My name was Ruth Foster then."

He watched her, trying to think back.

"I always wore pigtails."

He remembered, then, the long black pigtails that always got dunked in the ink well.

"Yes, Ruth, I remember. That's been a long time ago."

"It seems so now, doesn't it?"

There was a pause, and Jed stumbled ahead. "About your husband, did he tell you anything that might help us?"

She touched her temples with her suntanned hand. "I've told Mr. McIntosh everything I thought mattered. He did tell me not to trust the marshal in Hendersonville, the one who is a brother to Everett

Partlow." She thought a moment more. "Harold did say something about needing to make a report to Mr. McIntosh. But he never told me what it was about."

"Did he say he worked for the state or the governor?"

"Oh, no. He did say he was joining the Cattleman's Association. He showed me his card once and told me to keep it. I've still got it, I think." She rose and went to a highboy. In a moment, she came back with a small card. On it was printed a name, Harold Vanderzanden, the date, January 1869, and below a title, Special Investigator.

Jed pointed to the words, and she gasped.

"I never noticed that part before!"

Jed looked at it again. "At least we have one more clue to work with. Did your husband say where he was when they shot him?"

She stood and walked to the window, then came back.

"Yes, I know where they ambushed him. He said there were three of them, and they shouted to one another. Harold said he hid something out there, and I should try to find it after a month or so. He thought someone might be watching if I went back for it too quickly." She nodded. "I guess it's time. Wait here, I'll change into some riding clothes and be right back."

He started to say something, but she waved him quiet.

"Don't worry, I can take care of myself."

She came back quickly after dressing in a divided skirt and a yellow blouse with a doeskin vest over it. Strapped around her waist was a cartridge belt, and a small handgun nestled in a left-handed holster.

She pulled the weapon and checked the loads. The gun was a hybrid of some kind. Its handle was small, almost like a derringer, but the barrel was four inches long, and it was a revolver. It carried .44 slugs in the cylinder. She slipped it back in the holster.

"Hal made it for me," she said. "A regular .44 was too heavy for me."

She led the way outside and let Jed saddle a pinto for her. She stepped into the saddle quickly, and they rode north. They had gone only a mile from the house toward the river when Ruth Vanderzanden turned toward some rocks to the left of the trail. They stopped at the base of the rocks, and she took off the wide-brimmed hat and shook out her hair.

"Hal said three men ambushed him back

there on the trail. He was hit and scrambled up into these rocks."

Jed dropped from his horse and jumped onto the rocks. They were large ones, and Jed soon found a number of .45 caliber cartridges in the dirt. Near the same rock he found fresh scars and chips, which spelled a fight. Farther to one side he found a gray high-crowned hat. It had a bullet hole in it.

Jed went back to the bullet-marked rock and tried to figure out the angles. He looked over the lay of the land. If he had a squad that had to capture these rocks, how would he attack? Where would he put his riflemen? Directly in front, about one hundred yards away, stood a screen of hickory brush. To the left of that a small wash cut through, and to the other side a large oak tree grew.

He gave the hat to the widow and walked to the gully. In about the middle of it, he found some spent shell casings. Close by were three cigarette stubs and a half-empty Bull Durham sack. He kicked it, and it seemed heavy. Jed opened the sack and looked inside. It held five .44 shells, each with the lead noses cut deeply with an "X" — a dumdum bullet. When it hit anything it splattered, causing tremendous damage. He had seen some of them in the war. Some of the Union soldiers made their own. He pocketed the sack and traced the trench farther. Near the oak tree he found more shells, and another cigarette. The casings here were from a rifle.

Jed walked back to the girl.

He showed her what he had found and explained the dumdum bullets. She shuddered.

"You said something about coming back to get something?"

Ruth looked around the area, a frown of puzzlement on her pretty face.

"I'm not sure what he meant. He said to look under the rock. But which rock, there are hundreds around here?"

Jed thought about it. What would a dying man mean by that phrase, the rock? Which rock?

"Did the two of you ever come here?"

"Yes, quite often we had Sunday picnics here after church. There was a flat rock we used on the other side where it looks out over the valley."

Suddenly she was running, around the rocks, and Jed followed.

"One of the flat rocks we called 'The Rock' because we used it as a table!"

They found the spot. The big rock had

been firmed up with smaller rocks under one side. The slab was too heavy to lift. But whatever they were looking for might be pushed under the edge. They looked. Ruth found it. It was a long white envelope that had been folded twice to fit into a pocket. There was no address or name on the outside. It was sealed.

A rifle bullet slapped the rock beside them and whined away into the sky.

"Drop it nice and easy, and nobody gets hurt."

The voice, deep and low, came from the rocks above them.

Chapter Seven

Jed reacted without thinking. He pushed the girl roughly to the left behind a boulder and threw the envelope down the incline. As he dove for a rock to his right, the rifle snarled. Jed heard the bullet go past him; then he was under the overhang and out of sight.

He looked at Ruth and motioned for her to stay hidden.

"The letter is right down there. Go on down and get it!" Jed yelled at the gunman.

There was no reply. Jed motioned for the girl to stay where she was. She understood. He squirmed ahead, his gun in his hand. He reached back and took off his jangling spurs. In a minute or two, he had reached a higher rock that he could crouch behind. He could still see the white envelope on the cleared spot below. He moved faster and felt the rock slide under his foot. It made too much noise. He looked over at the rock where the rifleman had been. He was gone. Jed moved faster now and up the rocks toward the top. He found only one expended rifle cartridge.

Below, a denim-clad cowhand darted from the edge of the rocks for the envelope. He had to stop to pick up the paper. As he did, a gun fired twice. Jed lowered his own piece as he saw the man drop the letter and stab for his gun. His hand never made it. The man fell and rolled on his back. Jed knew he was dead before he got to the body. The two .44s both hit his chest, and a dark splotch grew on the man's shirt front.

Jed slipped the iron back in his holster and looked at Ruth. She sat on a rock, crying, her hands covering her face. Jed picked up the envelope and went back to her. He sat beside the small woman and touched her shoulder.

"That's all right, Ruth. You did what you had to do. Try not to think about it."

She leaned forward and touched him; she sobbed, and her body shook. Jed's arm came around her, and he held her like a little girl as she cried.

It was several minutes before she pulled away, and dabbed at her eyes. "I'm sorry,

Mr. Hart, I'm sorry. I — I — I never . . ."

He stood and helped her to her feet.

"I usually don't go to pieces that way." She wiped her eyes again and pulled some strands of hair away from her face.

"I've never killed anyone before." The tears started to come, but she blinked them back. "Harold said some day I might have to, to protect myself. But that man didn't even know I was there!"

Jed held both her shoulders tightly.

"Ruth, listen to me. If that man had reached that paper alive, he would have killed both of us if he could. Somehow that letter was worth a lot to him — or whoever he worked for." Jed let go of her. She was back in control.

He picked up the revolver and looked at it. It was a fine job of workmanship. The balance was good despite the appearance. He moved the cylinder to an empty chamber and pushed it into her holster.

Jed looked back at the man in the dirt. There was nothing they could do for him. If they left him there, the buzzards would pick his bones clean. But perhaps the man could tell them something after all. If he loaded the dead man on the horse and whacked it good, the cow pony would go straight home to its corral.

Jed took the envelope and tore open the end.

"I figure we got a right to know what's inside since we been shot at finding it."

The girl nodded and moved beside him as he unfolded the single sheet of paper. The message printed there made no sense.

"Send 23 Igloos to Eskimos. Enough Tents for Indians. 36985 98106 43297 54 32484 53 16798."

It was signed simply, "Happy."

They both stared at the message and the groups of numbers. Then Jed tucked the paper back into the envelope and put it inside the top of his boot.

"Reckon I should see that Corn McIntosh gets this delayed message, whatever it says."

Jed walked over to the body. He had never seen the man before. A quick search of his pockets showed six dollars in gold and some tobacco. There was no hint of any identity. Jed checked the six-gun rounds, but none had the ends of the slug cut up.

It took Jed almost five minutes of riding around the area to find where the horse of the dead man was tied. It was a quarter of a mile down a draw in a cluster of young cottonwoods. The horse had a Slash S brand on her hip. Jed untied her and soon had the gunman draped over the saddle. He used the lariat on the saddle to tie him securely to the stirrups.

Ruth had looked at the top of the rocks for the rifle and found it. They mounted, and Jed led the other horse as they moved back to the main trail.

"I can get home alone," she said. "Prince will be there."

He touched the brim of his hat in reply, and she started to ride off, then turned back.

"Jed, I'm not very good at making speeches. But I have a feeling things are going to be all right for me now. I just wished that . . ." She stopped and looked at him. "I wish you could have known Harold. He would have liked you, too." She turned and galloped down the trail toward her ranch.

Jed sat watching her go. Now he had another reason for finding out who killed Harold Vanderzanden.

He led the horse with its dead cargo almost to the edge of town before he whacked it on the rear with a rifle butt. The horse took off straight north, went around town, and slowed to a trot as it moved down the valley road. The only ranch in that end of the county was the Slash S.

It was not hanging evidence, but it sure fed the fires of Jed's suspicion. He turned northeast again, and for the first time realized it was almost dark. It was an hour later when he pulled up at Corn McIntosh's lake-front cabin.

Corn looked at the paper in the light of the kerosene lantern and grunted. He folded the message and put it back in the envelope. Jed put a few more sticks in the wood-burning cook stove and stirred a pot of beans.

"Corn, you old bushwhacker, what does the note mean?"

"Can't rightly say, Jed."

"Can't or won't?"

"Little of both. Hal Vanderzanden did bring messages to me from time to time. All I did was put them in another envelope and mail them. Hal was on special assignment for James M. Harvey, the honorable Governor of Kansas. That's all I can say."

"You knew Hal also worked for the Cattleman's Association?"

"I got him the job."

"And the two jobs kind of tied together?"

"Might, might not. Don't see how that's going to help you none trackin' down Vanderzanden's killer."

"There were three of them," Mrs. Vanderzanden said. " 'Pears now there are only two."

Corn shot tobacco juice out the door. "Figures they'd send a watchdog back who was in on the kill."

Jed slammed his fist down on the rough table, bouncing the light.

"It's got to be Partlow and the Slash S hired guns, but how can I prove it?"

"You can't right now," Corn said. He found an envelope in a box in the corner, addressed it, and put the Vanderzanden envelope inside. He handed it to Jed.

"Talk you into mailing that for me tonight on your way to your mother's house?"

"Might as well. It's too late already. They know what happened to Vanderzanden?"

Corn nodded.

Jed went to the stove and looked at the beans. "They done yet?"

"Done enough for a saddle bum on the grub line." He went to the bread box and dug out half a loaf of wheat bread and tossed it at Jed. "I suppose you want coffee and everything just like at a boarding house?"

Two hours later, Jed blended in with the shadows around the schoolhouse. He watched his mother's place for fifteen minutes more, and when he could find no evidence of anyone watching, he drifted from shadow to shadow around the school and across to the back of his mother's little house. He let himself in the back porch and opened the door into the kitchen silently. His gun was out of its home as he heard movement in the room. When he opened the door farther, he saw a woman washing her hair at the kitchen bench. It was Emily White. He did not know what to do. She had a towel around her shoulders, and her long blonde hair hung wet and soapy into a pan of water.

"Miss White?"

She screamed and straightened up; her hand caught the edge of the shallow pan, flipping it upside down, splashing water across the kitchen floor.

Emily White looked at him in fear and panic. Her wet blonde hair straggled across her face, and water dripped on the floor. For a moment, the surprise clung to her face; then, as she recognized him, the fear changed to anger, and she threw a bar of soap at him she still held.

"Jed Hart! What's the idea barging in here when I'm washing my hair? It's indecent."

"Miss White, it's my mother's house."

"You could have at least knocked on the front door like a gentleman."

"Then you would've had to bury me, Miss White, because I'd have ten slugs in my heart before you could get to the door." The irony in his voice was not lost on her. He picked up the pan and put it back in the big sink, pumping fresh water. He added some hot water to it from the teakettle on the wood stove.

"You'd better rinse that soap out of your hair before it dries. I'll clean up the mess on the floor."

Her eyes were cold and angry again. Her hair still dripped, and Jed wanted to laugh, but he did not. Somewhere there was a faint stirring in him about this girl. He found some rags and wiped the water off the boards of the kitchen floor. As he did, she stood with her hands on her hips for a moment, then bent and put her hair into the fresh rinse water. By the time he had the floor mopped, she was drying her hair.

"Where's my mother?"

90

"She went down the street to see a friend who is sickly."

"You want me to leave?"

The anger was gone from her eyes, and she tried a weak smile. "No, that isn't necessary." She laughed. "And I don't think you'll ever see me look any worse."

He smiled. "I'll look forward to my next visit." Their eyes met for a moment, and she glanced away.

"I'm sorry I was angry with you, but it was a real scare. People say we should keep a gun in the house, but I'm afraid of them. I've never shot one in my life."

Jed laughed. "Don't worry about that. Pretty schoolteachers never last very long in Hendersonville."

"What do you mean?"

"Some wild-eyed rancher comes down out of the prairie and marries them."

"Oh."

They heard the front door open and close. "Hello, Mrs. Hart, we've got company!"

His mother was crying before her arms went around him.

"Those horrid posters," she said.

"Ma, don't you worry none about them. Nobody's going to hurt me. I got help, Ma. Got a man who is helping me find out who the real killer was."

He held her away and helped her dry her tears.

"I keep seeing those awful posters, Jed. It scares me plumb to death. I tear down every one I see."

Jed laughed, and the tension was broken. "You be careful, Ma, or Partlow'll throw you in jail." He sobered. "Ma, did you get any bill of sale or title deed when you sold the ranch?"

She nodded. "Put 'em in the strong box in the sitting room. I'll get 'em."

She came back a moment later with a brown envelope. Inside was a title deed to the little house in town and a duplicate bill of sale that showed Mrs. Homer Hart accepted the sum of three hundred dollars and the town house in complete and full payment for the Double H cattle ranch, buildings, equipment, and livestock.

"It all looks legal, Ma, but I'll see what I can do."

"Jed, it won't do any good to try any legal maneuvering here in town, not as long as Partlow controls the marshal," Emily White said.

"I'm obliged for the advice, Miss."

Before she could reply, Mrs. Hart looked at Jed.

"Almost forgot, got a message for you.

Some little boy brought it to the door this afternoon."

Jed took the folded piece of paper from the sealed envelope. It was in a woman's hand:

"If you want to know who really killed Hal Vanderzanden, come to the Cattleman's and ask for Sarah."

He gave it to his mother to read.

"You sure ain't going to see her, Jed. She's a painted hussy. She cavorts around in that saloon half naked!"

Emily looked over Mrs. Hart's shoulder and read the note. She watched Jed, a smile on her face.

"You'll go, won't you, Jed?"

"Yes."

"Mrs. Hart, he has to go. There's nothing else for him to do. If this woman has some information that could help, it's very important to both you and Jed."

The older woman sat down in the rocking chair. "I keep forgetting you're a man now, Jed. Still think of you as almost eighteen, wantin' to go to war." She rubbed her forehead. "I lost you once, Jed. Now you're back safe. I don't want to lose you again."

Jed folded the papers to the ranch and house and tucked them inside his shirt.

"I'm going to see what I can do in court about this. Maybe we can do it all legal. But I doubt it." He looked at Emily White; she was still rubbing her hair with the towel.

"Next time I come calling, Miss White, I hope you at least have your hair combed." He grinned, and she smiled back. "I promise not to scare you." Jed patted his mother on the shoulder and went to the kitchen door. He opened it quickly and stepped onto the porch without a sound. A moment later, he dropped off the porch and ran for the clump of brush behind the house on a circuit toward his horse.

Chapter Eight

The Cattleman's Saloon was roaring when Jed edged up toward the front of it from the alley. He left his horse tied far back and came up the near wall in the shadows. He had no idea who Sarah was, except she was one of the dance-hall girls at the Cattleman's.

Jed waited by the side of the building until the man he wanted to see came down the boardwalk. He was about 60, had a limp, and was drunk. Jed recognized him as a loafer and a bum who had been hanging around the saloons six years ago. He grabbed the man's arm and pulled him into the dark alley.

"Don't hit me again. Don't hit me. What'd I do?"

Jed pinned him against the wall and let him mumble away his fright. When he calmed down, Jed took a dollar gold piece out of his pocket and waved it in front of the man's eyes.

"Like to have some gold, old man?" Jed watched the eyes gleam through half-closed lids.

"Take a note to Sarah for me. You know Sarah?"

The bloodshot eyes blinked, and the head nodded.

Jed tore in half the note that she had sent him and scribbled on the back of it: "Meet me in the alley." He signed it Jed.

Jed faded into the darkness and went to the alley behind the Cattleman's Saloon. The girls often slipped out that way with a friend after work or to get away from some overattentive cowboy. He waited ten minutes, and no one came.

Jed kicked the ground. He should not have trusted that old drunk. He slipped back along the buildings to the Cattleman's and tripped over something. It was his messenger, out cold.

Jed shook him awake and at last got the picture. Sarah did not work there anymore. She had gone to the hotel to pack. Jed dropped the man back to the dirt. It did not add up. The girls all lived over the saloon or in back. They did not live in the hotel. It smelled like a trap.

He shook the old man back to consciousness and got him on his feet.

"Old man, you take that note to Sarah in the hotel. Tell her it's urgent. If she won't come out, find out which room she's in."

Jed made the old man repeat the instructions back to him. Then he walked the drunk across the alley and up to the boardwalk. He aimed him across the street toward the hotel. The drunk walked with a drunken purpose through the ankle-deep dust in the street. He almost fell at the hotel door, but recovered and stumbled inside. Very quickly, the drunk came out and back to the alley. Jed faded into the shadows and watched, but no one followed the old man.

He slumped down at the sidewalk near the alley when Jed knelt beside him.

"Hotel deskman said she wouldn't come out."

"What room?"

"Room Twelve, second floor." He held out his hand, and Jed dropped the dollar gold piece into it, and the drunk passed out.

Getting to the second floor of the hotel from the outside was no problem. Jed climbed a fence and boosted to the first-floor roof from the fence. Only two lights showed in the second-story windows. Jed walked quietly to the first light. A man sat on the bed reading a dime novel. Jed went past it to the second window. A woman sat on a chair facing away from the window. She was neither young or old, but when she turned, he saw she wore cheek rouge and her lips were painted. She must be Sarah.

As Jed slid the window up, she turned and watched him. She waited until he was in the room, then stood. Sarah was taller than he had expected. Her arms were heavy, and her cheeks puffed too much. She wore the shimmering short gown that was the trademark of a cattleman's girl.

"Jed Hart?" she said.

He nodded, noting her husky voice.

"I don't like this town. I don't like the Partlows, and I'm on my way to California. Thought I could do you a favor." She smiled. "The man who killed Vanderzanden was one of the Slash S riders. Everybody called him Abe. He's a little blond guy, and his trigger finger's missing on his right hand."

"What's his last name, Sarah?"

"Don't know. You won't find him around here, anyway. They paid him off, and he rode south just after the gunplay."

"How do you know this, Sarah?"

"He told me. I helped him celebrate, and

he's got a big mouth."

Jed picked up her purse from the night stand and dumped it out on the bed. Five twenty-dollar bills fell out. Jed counted them and looked at her.

"Where did you get one hundred dollars?"

"I don't have to tell you."

Jed heard a door burst open behind him, and as he spun, he started to draw. The round, black hole of a six-gun aimed at his chest stopped him.

"Go on, Sarah, tell the nice man who done gave you that hundred dollars. Tell him, Sarah!"

The gun held steady on Jed's chest. The man laughed and watched Sarah pick up the contents of her purse and drop them inside.

The gunman looked at Jed now.

"Pleased to meet ya, Jed Hart. My name's Marshal Paul Partlow."

Chapter Nine

Paul Partlow did not resemble his brother. He stood tall and broad-shouldered. His face flushed, and his coat struggled to cover his large belly. His hand was fat around the six-gun.

"Just stand easy, Hart. I can use that three hundred dollars as well as anybody."

The corners of the town marshal's mouth pulled down in a sneer. "You're the saddle bum who's got Ev all riled up? Don't seem none too bright to me, or tough, either. Tell him, Sarah. Tell him how you and me worked this out. How I gave you that one hundred dollars to get him up here."

Sarah moved for the first time. She sat down on the bed and glared at the marshal.

"You lie, Partlow. I never talked to you about Jed." Partlow motioned with his gun at Jed. "Just toss your iron on the bed. I want you alive and talkin'."

Jed took the gun out of its holster slowly and put it on the bed.

"No hard feelings, Sarah," Jed said. "A hundred dollars is a lot of money."

"But I never talked to that scum!" She stood waving her arms, her face flushed.

"Sarah, honey, you don't need to cover up. Shore I said I wouldn't tell, but so what?"

"Hey!" Sarah bellowed. "You hiding in my closet all the time. You watched me undress and everything!"

"Stop it, Sarah. Lots of guys in town seen you in the altogether!"

When Partlow glanced back to Jed a second, she rushed him. The surprise was total. Sarah was clawing at his face with her long nails before he knew she was moving. She slammed into him and Partlow let out a grunt and tried to step away. She slashed at him with her hands, ripping new furrows down his cheeks. One of her hands slammed into Partlow's gun arm and the Colt dropped to the floor and discharged with a roar.

Jed leaped toward his own weapon as soon as Partlow lost his. Jed scooped up his gun and jumped toward the lawman, who had turned to defend himself from Sarah.

The barrel of Jed's six-gun slammed against Partlow's head, and he slumped to the floor.

Sarah watched him fall and kicked him in the stomach. She was about to kick him again when Jed took her arm and guided her to one side.

"Easy, Sarah. I know how you feel, but slow down."

Sarah sat on the edge of the bed, her breath coming fast, her eyes still angry at the man on the floor. Jed took the lawman's belt and wrapped it around his ankles. He ripped a pillow case into strips and tied the marshal's hands and gagged him.

Sarah still sounded as mad as a wet prairie chicken.

"Jed, I didn't do what he said."

"I know, Sarah. I know. What will you do now?"

"Meaning what?"

"You can't stay in town. The marshal will throw you in jail for helping me. Stage left about sundown, so you can't go out that way until tomorrow."

She rubbed her forehead. "Me and my big yap. What if that John did see me change clothes? Ain't like I was a virgin. Hell, I don't know what I'm gonna do." A sly smile spread over her face. "You got a camp, a cabin? You need a cook?"

"No cabin." He watched her.

"Hear tell you been stayin' with Corn McIntosh. He's got a cabin. Nice little place up by the lake."

Jed laughed. He had forgotten how quickly news traveled in a small town.

"Corn would blow his cork."

"Would you rather see me in jail? You got me into this mess. I was trying to help you."

Jed knew she was afraid. Paul Partlow would throw away the key to her cell.

"We can ride out and ask Corn."

"It's a deal!"

"You got any riding clothes?"

"You bet." She flipped open a carpetbag and began rummaging in it.

"Maybe I better leave until you get dressed."

"Suit yourself." She was already unfastening the buttons at the back of her dress.

Jed stepped out the window onto the roof and hunkered down against the wall. The street below was quiet. He watched the men striding along the boardwalks. It was easy to tell the townsmen from the ranch hands. Almost none of the townsmen wore guns. It had been a long time now since he had lived without a gun.

A few minutes later, Sarah's head poked out the open window.

"Let's move, Jed. This big ape is coming around, and I don't want to be here when he starts banging on the floor."

Before they left Jed kicked the marshal's gun under the bed.

On the long ride to Corn McIntosh's cabin, Jed found out a lot about Sarah. She had been born and raised on a ranch near town and had learned to rope and ride as well as her brothers. Then, when the Slash S moved in with guns and the torch, her Pa had been killed and her mother hurt, and the boys drifted. She was left to look out for herself.

"That was three years ago. I've been taking care of myself since." She tilted her chin up and looked at him. "It ain't what you'd call a very nice life, but at least I'm still alive."

Before they left town, Jed had roused the bartender at the Pastime to provide a second horse. It was saddled and ready within minutes. Jed had tied Sarah's two carpetbags onto the back of the saddle.

Now they splashed through the narrow opening of the little valley and rode around the lake. Corn did not come out when they stopped by the tie rail. The cabin was dark.

"I got a shotgun on both of ye. Better stay put till I know who's callin'."

"It's Jed, Corn. We got company."

They swung down from the horses, and in a few moments Corn had the lamp lit. When he saw the woman, he swore.

"Sarah, what in tarnation you doin' here? No, no, don't tell me. You're feudin' with the Partlows again, and Jed here offered to take you in. He picks up stray dogs the same way. I'd have a corral full if I could saddle the dern things. You can stay tonight, but first thing in the morning we'll flag down the stage and put you aboard!"

Sarah shook out her dark hair and grinned at the angry face.

"Corn, how would a mess of fried potatoes and onions sound, along with a batch of fresh biscuits and gravy? How about some warm bread, heaped up with butter and preserves? I hired on as head cook, and that's what I'm gonna be!"

Corn snorted and tossed her carpetbag onto the porch.

"Women is a dang nuisance. Don't need them 'tall." Corn paused and sent a long stream of dark juice into the night.

"You say fried potatoes smothered with onions?"

Sarah nodded.

Corn sighed. "That sure sounds good." He frowned and kicked at the corner of the porch. "Well, fer kittenfish sakes, guess it won't hurt none fer you to stay fer a spell."

Sarah kissed his grizzled cheek and ran into the cabin.

"Why in tarnation you bring a woman here?"

"She told me who killed Harold Vanderzanden, Corn. And Marshal Partlow heard her and was taking me in. She jumped him and I got away. I couldn't just leave her there."

"Say she told you who killed Hal?"

"One of the Slash S riders who moved on the next day."

"Leastwise we know now for sure."

"But that won't do us much good, Corn. I'm aimin' to do something positive. Goin' to Coldwater and find me an honest lawyer and file a lawsuit. See if I can get the ranch back that way. If it don't help, I ain't out but fifteen dollars and a long ride."

Corn mumbled as they went inside. They sat at the rough plank table.

"Pure waste o' time going all that way to Coldwater. Bunch of lawyer talk ain't gonna do no good."

"Least it's in the next county where most of our Double H ranch was. The Partlows can't stop me, and the judge might see it my way."

Corn spat at the bucket sitting in the corner of the cabin. Sarah grabbed the bucket and tossed it through the door.

"You want to spit, you go outside with the horses."

Jed laughed, and Corn turned purple, but held his tongue. It was a truce of sorts. Jed started getting ready for his ride. Since the "Wanted" posters were out on him, he would be traveling at night. That meant right now.

Sarah put together two days' worth of food for him and some cooking gear. He unsaddled the horses they rode in and looked over the string Corn kept in the corral. He picked a chestnut that looked like she had lots of staying power. Jed brushed her down carefully and put the blanket on, then the saddle. He dropped a Spencer rifle in the scabbard. The rifle was like the one he had used in the war. It held seven shots with a .56 caliber slug that could knock down a horse at half a mile. When his blanket roll and grub sack had been tied on securely, Jed was ready to move.

"Bunch of darn foolishness," Corn snorted. "Just a two-day waste of time."

"Got to try, Corn. Way I figure, we got laws, so I'll try to use them. If that don't work, then I might have to make some laws of my own."

Sarah held up a last cup of coffee. "You don't pay no mind to what Corn says. Everybody knows he's a stick-in-the-mud. We'll look for you day after tomorrow. But you take care. That three hundred dollars is pullin' in lots of gun trash."

Jed tipped his hat at Sarah and touched spurs to the side of the chestnut. She moved out eagerly, as if she were glad the fussing was over and she could get going.

Jed turned almost due north across the hills and up the gentle slope toward the county seat of Comanche County. Coldwater was not a city, but bigger than Hendersonville. They had over five hundred people there.

Coldwater was on the back trail to Dodge City another forty-five miles on north and west. Jed judged the distance he had to cover at thirty miles each way. It was nearly midnight by the stars when Jed let the chestnut out into a gentle mile-eating lope. He wanted to cover as much of the ground as he could before daylight — about six hours away. But he had to keep his mount fresh enough to withstand a good chase if somebody challenged him. That should not come until daylight, though, and by then he would be in the next county.

He angled to the northwest. It took him one ridge behind the Double H. No time to check out the house now. On a long grassy meadow, he let the chestnut run. She responded with a hard gallop for half a mile, and Jed pulled her back down. She had good speed.

He came to a slight rise and paused to let the horse blow. He quieted her and listened, but heard no hoof beats either way, and no sound came except some night birds. A look at the stars told Jed it was nearing two o'clock. It had been a long time since he had ridden all night.

Kicking the chestnut into motion, Jed settled her into a lope that had moved them well. He estimated they had covered ten miles the first two hours. Another ten miles and he would be far enough out of Barbour County to relax. He eased the six-gun up and down in the holster and splashed across a small stream. Jed stopped to check his direction. The moon gave him a good view of the low line of hills ahead. The route would be uphill most of the way now. There was no trail, not even a deer path to follow.

Jed saw the notch in the hills and angled toward it, following the stream that seemed to work its way toward the pass. The country was drier here, but the grass seemed the same. There were more oak and hickory groves on the slopes and fewer of the cottonwoods that clustered mainly around the streams.

He let his mount drink at a creek, and in a few moments of silence a two-point buck deer pranced to the stream fifty yards away and drank. When he caught the human smell, the deer bounded away into the brush.

In the daytime, he would see tracks of antelope and elk here as well as buffalo, turkey, and beaver. But he was not hungry now.

He urged the mare ahead faster, trying to maintain his five-mile-per-hour speed, but he knew that he was falling behind. Someday, this whole country would be laced with railroads, he thought. You could buy a ticket and ride anywhere you wanted to go on the thin rails of steel. But that was not now. He touched spurs to flanks and urged the chestnut up the slope.

When the stars told him that it was four a.m., Jed dropped off the horse and ground-tied her before he pulled down the bedroll and grub sack. An early breakfast and a nap would feel good.

He built a small fire, keeping it as smokeless as possible, and boiled some coffee and put slabs of jerky between biscuits. Jed ate with surprising hunger. It was sleep he would be needing more than food if he did not get some soon. When he finished eating, he rolled out the blanket and eased the cinch on the chestnut. She would be happy that way for a couple of hours.

Jed kicked dirt over the fire and stretched out. The Spencer nestled near his leg, and his .44 lay beside his right hand. He never knew when he went to sleep.

Jed woke with a start, and the .44 was in his hand. He fired a shot in the air. It was morning, and a man had been rummaging in his grub sack.

"Morning, friend," the stranger said. "Hated to wake you up." The voice came from a man in his thirties who was unshaved and almost bald. His eyes were dark and his clothes in need of washing and repair. He had been eating. Jed rose and moved toward him carefully. The man had no gun showing.

"Who are you?" Jed asked.

"People call me Oliver. Just Oliver. Look, didn't mean no harm. Smelled your smoke and thought you might share vittles with me. Am a mite hungry."

"You on the grub line?"

Oliver laughed and drew his fingers across his nose. "Shore am. Long as it don't mean no work and long as it don't mean no sheriff. Me and the law don't get on none too good."

"But you saw no cause to shoot a sleeping man just for his grub and horse?"

" 'Pears as how, Mister, 'cause my brother Harry got a gun lookin' at your spine right now."

Jed heard the scuff of a boot and a six-gun cocked behind him. He dove to the left, rolled, drew, and fanned his left palm across the hammer of his gun three times so fast it almost sounded like one explosion.

Jed had seen only a vague shape when he fired. Now he stood slowly, six-gun still ready, and watched the man on the ground. A red splotch below the cowboy's left shirt pocket marked one bullet. Another had shattered his elbow. His arm lay at a strange angle across his dirty blue shirt. A low-crowned gray hat tilted across his head, showing black hair and two hard black eyes under full brows. The man's breath came in wheezing gasps, and the one who said he was Oliver ran over and eased his head to the ground.

"You had no cause to shoot Jason!"

"A cocked pistol at my back is cause aplenty."

The man on the ground blinked his eyes and watched Jed. He coughed and there was a light red froth at his lips.

"Told you, Oliver. Should oughta just shot him." The man on the ground groaned, and his eyes rolled back. He coughed again, spilling red saliva out of his mouth.

Jed watched Oliver closely, his gun ready. They were gun trash, and from the sound of their accent, they were from the South. A few years ago, Jed may have fought against these men.

"Hold it!" Jed ordered as Oliver's hand moved toward the pocket of his jacket. "Lay the derringer on the ground."

"I got no gun."

Jed cocked the iron in his hand, and Oliver swallowed.

"Lay it out, now!" Jed's hand jogged a fraction of an inch, and the gun fired a slug through Oliver's sleeve.

"O.K., don't get trigger happy," Oliver

said, putting a two-shot hand gun on the ground. He pushed the dying man away and stood. "Can I ride out of here?"

"What about your brother?"

"He's no kin of mine. Met up with him a week ago. We saw this 'Wanted' poster yesterday and decided to look around a bit." He kicked at the dirt. "Well, to me three hundred dollars is most two years steady working pay."

"Why you looking through my gear?"

"Jason made me do it. Said he wanted to be sure you was this Jed Hart before we gunned you."

At the sound of his name, the wounded man turned his head toward them. His eyes blinked and then closed. He gave a sigh that sounded like the wind through a cottonwood tree late at night, and his head rolled back.

An hour later, Oliver and Jed stepped back from the mound of rocks and wiped the sweat off their faces. The grave had been covered with rocks.

Jed stripped the shells out of the derringer and checked Oliver's saddlebags for more bullets. He found a box and took it, then ordered the man on his horse.

"And don't come back. My Spencer will

trail you a mile and a half. You better keep goin' after that."

" 'Pears as how I will, Mr. Hart. No hard feelings?"

For an answer, Jed slapped the horse on the flank, and it galloped down the slope into the valley. Jed sent a rifle bullet beside the horse and watched it pick up speed.

It was noon before Jed pulled into Coldwater. It looked like Hendersonville, but had two main streets and a few other cross streets. There were more shops and houses and more people.

Jed rode down the main street, watching signs on both sides. He saw one lawyer's sign, but it was old, and the office looked too prosperous. The next sign he saw pointed upstairs over one of the saloons. Jed tied his horse to the rail and took the steps two at a time.

"David B. Van Pelt, Attorney at Law," the sign on the door read. Jed turned the knob and went in.

A neat daybed sat against one wall, with a dresser and small cupboard at the far back. In the front of the room, facing the door, stood a large oak desk. Jed wondered how they squeezed it through the door. The man behind the desk stood up.

"My name is Van Pelt, David B. Van Pelt. And I have explicit instructions to take you into custody and remand you to the town marshal at Hendersonville."

Jed's hand seemed hardly to move, but the gun was suddenly out and the sights centered on Van Pelt's chest.

"Yes, I can see by your gun work you must be Jed Hart. Marshal Partlow from Hendersonville said you might come over here to enter a fraudulent claim against some property purchased from your mother."

The lawyer was young, not over twenty-four, Jed guessed. He dressed elegantly, his hair pomaded, and he probably washed three or four times a day. But he was smiling and held out his hand.

"That's what your marshal said. We're not impressed here with Partlow. Sit down, rest yourself. I hope you brought the bill of sale, the adjusted true value of the land, and any other important papers."

Jed grinned at the young man. He was a quick judge of men, and he knew this type. He had seen dozens of them in the war. Men who could talk your arm off, swear at you, and fight with you one minute, and an hour later give up their lives for your safety.

The dusty cowboy dropped a packet of papers onto the desk and holstered his gun.

"I reckon we might do some business, Mr. Van Pelt. And I'm in a bit of a rush."

Chapter Ten

The following afternoon, Jed swung down from his horse at Corn's cabin, tired and saddle-sore. After pulling the saddle off the chestnut, he gave her a feeding of oats and yahooed her into the corral. Then it was time to think about his own feed.

The smell of fresh bread drifted across his path as he walked to the main room of the cabin.

"Welcome back, Jed!" Sarah said. Her hair had been piled high on her head, and she wore a print dress with ruffles around the throat and at the cuffs. Her face was flushed, and she motioned at the three loaves of bread and pan biscuits on the table.

"Sure hope you don't like warm bread or we might not have enough left for supper."

She laid out a dish of freshly made plum jam and a bread knife for Jed. Jed measured off two inches on the loaf and sawed through.

Between bites, he told Sarah what happened on his trip.

"So it looks like I made a long ride for nothing, just like Corn said." Jed looked around. "Where is Corn?"

Sarah took the last bread pan from the oven of the wood-burning cook stove and expertly tipped the loaf out and rolled it over to cool.

She touched the corner of her apron to moisture on her forehead and sat down.

"Corn took off on the stage two days ago. Said he had to go to the state capitol to do some business." She grinned at Jed with open appreciation. "But I bet it was some monkey business."

Jed finished the slab of bread and looked at the loaf, then stood up.

"Think I'll take my blanket roll out under those trees and catch myself a short snooze. Wake me up if Corn comes back." He was about to go out the door when she touched his arm.

"Jed, I wanted to tell you what I told the others." She paused and watched his face before she went on, her eyes not holding his now. "You know where I worked and all. But I say a girl has a right to change her mind. And I have. Soon as I can, I'm moving on to a new town and start all over.

I can cook in a boardin' house or clerk in a store to make my living. Maybe someday I can even get married." She watched him closely now, and he nodded. "I told the rest of the men and Corn. Just wanted to tell you."

"I'll keep my eye out for a bachelor rancher who likes homemade bread and plum jam." He grinned as he said it and headed for his blanket roll.

When Jed left two days before, only Corn and Sarah had been at the place. Now a lean-to perched against the back of the structure, and two cowboys lounged near the corral. They nodded, and Jed noticed that each of them carried a gun, and both looked like they could use the weapons.

A few minutes later, Jed lay on his stomach under the trees, watching the trail at the far end of the lake. He pounded his hand against the ground in frustration. He felt he was no further along now than when he came to town that first day. He knew more about what was going on; he knew for sure now who his enemies were; he knew who it was who had tried to pin a murder on him. But knowing and doing were different trails. He had to do something! He had to make the Partlows know he was fighting.

Jed knew what Corn would say — that being still alive was something. Jed pulled clover blossoms off a clump and began sucking the sweet juices from the white blossoms.

What could he do? Call out Ev Partlow and gun him down? He would get backshot before he could go for his gun. Same thing held for Ben Matheson. But he had to strike back at them somehow!

If he had a platoon of riflemen, he could move in and wipe out the Partlow ranch and take over the marshal's office. Only this was not a war. Not even a small range war. But could it be? Could he find enough of the people who Ev Partlow had run out and scared off their land to throw in with him now and fight the Partlow crew? It would give him something to work on, some support from more residents. When real law came to the valley, Jed had no desire to be a wanted man again. He stood up and rolled the blanket before walking back toward the cabin. A glint of sun on metal caught his eye at the far end of the lake, and Jed saw two riders rounding the water and heading for the cabin. One of them was Corn, the other probably one of the new hands who had trailed a horse for Corn to ride when he dropped off the stage at Buckets Crossing.

A moment later, Corn swung off the horse carefully and gave the reins to the other rider. Corn looked about the same, just a little dirtier, Jed thought.

"See ya made it."

"True," Jed said.

"Hanker to clear the dust out of your throat before supper?"

Jed said he would, and they moved inside where Corn took out the brown and white jug with its corncob stopper. As the jug went back and forth, Jed told Corn about his trip to Coldwater and the problems he had on the way. The unenthusiastic response of the young lawyer did not surprise Corn.

"Fer kittenfish sakes, least you tried."

"Hear you went to the capitol. Must have been a quick trip, all that way in just two days."

Corn laughed and tipped the jug again. "Fact is I telegraphed the capitol from Wichita. They got a safe wire there."

"Corn, I hear quite a few men been run out of their land by Partlow. Any of them still around who might want to fight him?"

Corn screwed up his face and pulled at his dirty chin whiskers. "Three of 'em were shot dead; two that I know moved out of the state. Must be four or five around. I could get word to them through the Pastime if you wanted to talk to them."

"Five men — that'd be a start. See if you can get in touch with them. Like to contact as many as will come to Buckets Crossing in the morning."

Corn turned and sent a stream of tobacco juice toward the spittoon that usually sat in the corner next to the stove.

Sarah howled and stormed at Corn with a wet cloth she had been using on her baking pans.

"Corn, that's the third time you done that. Your dirty old spittoon is outside where it belongs! I told you it's either that spit pot or my cooking."

Jed and Corn walked outside, and Corn sent another stream of brown juice over the porch rail.

"That's better," Sarah said from the door. She grinned and her anger dissolved. "Supper in half an hour — if you like venison steak and mashed potatoes and gravy."

Corn found one of his hands, and soon the man saddled up and rode for town.

The next morning Jed crouched behind a screen of hickory and watched two riders come into the shade at Buckets Crossing and let their horses drink. They dismounted, started a small cooking fire, and set out three coffee cups on a stump. That was the sign he had been waiting for. Jed came out of concealment and walked down to the men.

The first was a rangy man, nearly six feet, loose-jointed, with a square jaw and a hint of anger in his eyes. He took Jed's hand with a firm grasp.

"Granger," the man said, and looked at Jed. "I'm glad to be here."

"Armstrong, Clint Armstrong, Mr. Hart," the second man said. "Mighty glad to come. Hope we can do something about the Partlows. Burned me out one night, run off my stock. Next day some of his hands run me and the family off the place."

The talker was shorter than Jed by a head and slight. He did not wear a gun, but a rifle stuck out of the boot of his saddle. He wore overalls and a battered felt hat. Jed guessed Armstrong was as much farmer as cowman.

Jed talked to the two men for half an hour, explaining his position, telling them what he had lost and suggesting that they all get together and try to outthink the Partlows.

"What about the marshal?" Granger asked.

"I talked that over with a lawyer friend of mine," Jed replied. "He tells me the marshal is a town marshal — hired by the town. He's got no jurisdiction or power at all outside the city limits. Real lawman in the county is the sheriff. I wondered why some of you men didn't go to the county sheriff over in Medicine Lodge."

"You found out in a rush, I bet," Armstrong said.

"I hear that Partlow got the sheriff elected — a political deal. Now anything that Partlow wants done or not done, the sheriff thinks is just fine."

"So to get some real law in here it'll take a U.S. marshal," Jed finished.

"And they are hard to get hold of," Granger said. "I spent two months trying to get one in here to clean this mess out."

"So we have to do it ourselves," Jed went on. "We may have to fight fire with fire. Get enough things going and we might do it. Whittling away at Partlow everywhere we can."

"You're talkin' range war, Mister," the shorter man said.

"Ev Partlow isn't going to roll over and play dead just because we tell him to,

Armstrong. You know that as well as me. So we meet force with force. The Partlow boys understand that."

"Count me in, Jed," Granger said. His tall frame tightened a bit as he spoke. "When Partlow raiders burned me out, they got the house first. Wife and kids ran to the barn to hide. When the raiders burned the barn, they didn't have a chance to get away. I got nothing to lose anymore."

Jed watched Armstrong take off his hat and scratch his stringy brown hair.

"Mr. Hart, I don't aim to get mixed up in a range war. I still got a wife and three kids. But I shore would like to get my land back." He curled the rim of his hat and looked at it. When he glanced up, there was strength in his face.

"Mr. Hart, I'll work with you long as there's no killin'. If there's killin', I'll have to think it through again."

"Armstrong, I got no intentions of shootin' up the Partlows for sport. I don't like killing men any more than you do. But somebody is bound to get hurt before this is over. You better pick your side right now. You go with us all the way, or you get behind your wife's petticoats right now."

The short man slapped his hat against

his leg twice and then nodded. "O.K. I'm with you."

Before noon, Jed had talked with two more men; they both "signed on" in the fight with Partlow. They were told they would be notified about the next step.

Back at the cabin that noon, Jed put it up to Corn. "You said you would help me. Does that include ten gun hands?"

Corn pulled his whiskers and smoothed his moustache.

"Ten guns? You aimin' to hold up a bank?"

Jed didn't answer, and Corn watched Sarah fussing around the stove. He turned back to Jed, his shaggy head nodding.

"By jangles, I reckon we can scrape up ten men. You sure don't ask for little things when you ask. Who is gonna pay those gun hands?"

"I will, soon as I get the ranch working."

"Gun hands don't work for promises. They cost forty dollars a head hard money a month. You good for four hundred a month?"

Jed shook his head.

"I am. They'll be here tomorrow morning ready to ride."

"Can you tell those four ranchers, too?"

"They're counted in the ten."

Jed showed surprise. "Well, I guess two to one odds aren't so bad."

"Lots better than the last time you took on Partlow."

"How's that?"

"Last time it was twenty to one."

"We're going to do more than threaten him this time."

Jed began his planning in earnest. He talked with Sarah and planned out how they could send along two days' hard food with each man in saddlebags. She helped him work out a list of staples they would need at the Double H for housekeeping, sugar, flour, bacon, jerky, etc.

At supper that night, Corn McIntosh jumped up and kissed Sarah when she served him sauerkraut and ham hocks.

"Now where did you get sauerkraut?"

"My secret," Sarah said, beaming. "But I hope you don't stop by at Ma Jackson's boarding house for supper."

Jed could not remember eating so well since he left home for the army. Sarah brought out scalloped potatoes with cheese, a venison roast, and baked beans. For dessert, they had baked apples.

Corn leaned back in his chair and belched.

Sarah grinned and winked. "A good belch is a sign of a good dinner, Corn. I thank you."

The three cowboys excused themselves and drifted out to the front porch where a whist game soon developed.

Corn eyed Jed finishing his second slice of venison.

"You eat like you won't see food for a month," Corn chided.

"I might not, and this is one of my last of Sarah's dinners," Jed explained.

"What in tarnation you aimin' to do to-morrow with your eleven gunmen?"

"Since it's your money, you got a right to ask, Corn. We're taking and holding the Double H ranch buildings. By the time Partlow finds out about it, we'll be dug in so deep he'll never blast us loose."

The new day dawned crisp and clear. Jed sent one of the cowboys into town with the list of staples and told him to buy a light wagon to haul them in. He was to get his load and bring it back as far as Buckets Crossing and wait. He was to bring back the four ranchers with him.

Corn sent another of his men into town to alert the other three gun hands and bring them back to the cabin. There was not much to do. The rations were packed in saddlebags and in gunny sacks for the townsmen. Guns were cleaned, and Jed took a nap.

Two hours after supper, Jed had inspected his five men and moved out toward Buckets Crossing. The wagon and the five men waited for them. Soon they turned north toward the Double H spread. Jed asked Granger to come up front with him.

"You in the war, Granger?"

The tall man nodded in the soft moonlight.

"Figured we need to have a second in command. Suit you?"

"Suits me."

"Tonight we want to take the Double H ranch and hold it. We put up some barricades if we have time and settle in like we mean to hold it. We do."

They rode for a distance in silence.

"Long-range plan is like we talked yesterday. We nick him here and siphon off a few head of his steers. We hit him somewhere else — maybe burn down a barn or a line shack. We irritate him until the Slash S does something criminal that we can prove. Then we grab them and the evidence and one of us rides for Wichita and a U.S. marshal."

"Still figure there'll be some killin'?"

"Bound to be, Granger."

Clouds scudded over the moon as they rode. By ten o'clock, they were still three miles from the Double H. Jed separated the group, then took half the men with him and left the other half with Granger. Jed would move in quickly and take over the buildings. He did not expect more than two or three riders there.

They walked their animals the last half mile and tied them up below the barn. The five men moved quickly into the building and found two horses. Jed sent two men to the back of the house and took two with him to the kitchen door. The men had bunked in the kitchen before; these probably would do the same.

Jed paused at the door and listened. One snore came through loudly. He opened the door and stepped inside. Two forms sprawled on the floor under blankets.

He whispered to one of the men to light a lamp. It burned brightly before the first man woke.

"What in tarnation?"

Jed's six-gun stopped the question as it nuzzled into the puncher's neck. They kicked the other hand awake.

"You both Slash S hands?" Jed asked.

"Shore are, Mister. We heard you booted some of our boys off here. Man, were they mad after walking home! Ben fired them same day."

"That sounds like Ben. You two want to go back to Partlow?"

The second wrangler shook his head. "He'd just beat us up before he fired us. We thinkin' of moving south a bit, maybe to New Mexico."

"Forking Slash S stock?"

They both nodded. "Would you say it's a fair trade for the animal you rode in on when you signed?"

Both heads bobbed.

Jed took ten dollars in paper money from his pocket and gave each man five.

" 'Less you want to get in a range war, you saddle up and ride quick. Get out of the county tonight, and don't come back."

Jed sent one man with them to be sure they packed and saddled quickly; then he rounded up all the lamps he could find. They cleaned out the kitchen a little — and the dining room.

Two men went out as sentries, one down the town road, the other toward the Slash S. Jed was sitting down to a cup of hot coffee in the kitchen when the wagon and the other five hands pulled in.

As they unpacked, Granger asked how it went. Jed told him. "Now let's get some sleep. Tomorrow we've got to figure how to defend this place."

Chapter Eleven

Jed slipped out the kitchen door and moved ahead to the well. He sat on the stone foundation and rubbed his face with his hands. Most of the men had settled down in beds or blankets. Three were out on guard now, and relief would ride out just before daylight.

He glanced up at the starry time clock in the sky. It was a little after one a.m. They had put in a good night's work, but he knew he could not sleep. The idea of being back on the home spread was enough to keep him stirred up all night.

He pulled a bucket of water up from the hand-dug well. Jed remembered digging it with his pa. They had gone down sixty feet before they came to the right kind of sand.

Jed swished the water in his mouth before he swallowed it. Best water in the valley.

The last lamp in the kitchen went out

before Jed settled against the well. It was cooler there. He took off his hat and curled up the edges to a right angle. Maybe he could rest his eyes for just a moment, he thought, and leaned back against the stone of the well.

The noise to his left brought Jed half awake, and he reached for his .44, but something blinded him. He shook his head, and as his eyes cleared, he saw the sun beating into his eyes over the barn.

Three men had just dismounted and pulled saddles off their horses. After the animals trotted into the corral, the men turned to the kitchen, both hungry and sleepy.

One man had been named cook and had the breakfast coffee hot and ready. They would eat out of their saddlebags today. Jed called Granger, and they looked over the spread from a high point just in back of the house.

"Figure we can put up some kind of a barricade between the small corral and the barn and another one from the barn to the haystack," Jed suggested.

Granger nodded. "What we got to build with?"

"One wagon in the barn, maybe two by

135

now, and we can cut some poles up the hill."

Together they laid it out in a crude square, with the well, the house, and a fenced garden making up the other three sides. Granger flexed his hands.

"I'll get some men and secure the far side. Then we'll work on those poles and fence."

Jed watched the tall man walk away. Granger had been a good choice for his second.

They worked hard all morning. Before the sun topped its arch, the lookout from the west came galloping into the yard.

"Four riders coming, Jed. Looks like they're from the Slash S."

"How far out?"

"About three miles. Riding easy."

"Go back and shadow them in. Keep out of sight. When you're sure they're coming here, blast back and tell us."

Jed moved the work to the back of the square and kept it quiet. They had a rough but sturdy fence built from the haystack to the well and on past to the edge of the house before the rider came back.

"Not more'n five minutes out, Jed."

"O.K. men. Quit work and get out of sight. Get the rifles out, and be ready to use them. We should surprise them. No shooting unless I give you the word."

They slid into the barn, under the corral, and in the house. Not a man could be seen when the four riders trotted past the corral.

All wore guns and straddled Slash S stock. The lead man seemed to be in charge. He looked questioningly at the fence by the well, but he was in the trap by then.

"Hold it right there!" Jed yelled from a window of the house. "We've got twenty guns on you, so drop your iron into the dirt."

None of the men moved; the three looked at the lead man for a hint. He paused, then drew and slapped a shot at the window.

Jed's rifle had followed the draw, and when the man's hand came up, the rifle cracked. The round smashed the gunman's hand and toppled him off the horse.

The rest of the riders dropped their six-guns without an argument.

"Get off your horses and sit down on the ground," Jed called. He vaulted through the open window, covering the group with his six-gun. Others came from hiding. They watched silently as the wounded man tore off his neckerchief and tried to bandage his bleeding hand. Jed took the cloth and bound the hand tightly to stop the flow of red.

"You're on private property," Jed said.

"This is Slash S land," the stranger said.

Jed shook his head. "The Sein Valley Cattleman's Protective Association doesn't agree. This is the Double H spread owned by the Hart family. We've got twenty guns to back up what we say. How many have you got?"

Jed turned and looked at the other three men.

"How long each of you been working the Partlow spread?"

Two of them had been on the payroll a month, the other for six months.

"You know what happened to those two Slash S men who walked home without their mounts?" The three nodded. "Now the same thing might happen to you unless you want to turn and ride south for the Indian Territories or on into Texas."

"Give up our jobs?"

"Would you rather walk back to the Slash S and tell Ben that you lost your mount? Lost it to Jed Hart?"

The two youngest men wiped the dust from their eyes and looked at each other.

They shrugged, whispered a minute.

"Might just as well ride south, sir. I'm not going to let that crazy Ben beat me up."

"And you?" Jed asked the other two.

One said he would go south; the other one hedged and then scowled.

"I don't see no twenty guns around here."

"Next time you see them, friend, it will be when they spout gunsmoke. Now you riding or walking?"

"I'm not running out. I want to see Ben gutshot you and then pull your fingernails out."

Jed turned to the wounded man. "You want to go into town to see the doc or run home to Ben?"

"I better see the doc."

"You'll have to ride alone unless you can talk one of these boys into going with you." Jed stripped the bullets out of the men's guns and tossed them back.

"You three, mount up and ride before I change my mind." Jed motioned to the mounted lookout who trailed the men out of camp down the town road.

The fourth man flexed his hands, watching Jed.

"How about my gun?" he asked.

Jed had held it when he returned the others. He tossed it to the man. "You've got a long walk, wrangler, you better get moving."

A half hour later the men had eaten jerky and biscuits, washing the food down with coffee before they went to work.

Jed watched the work and estimated the time they had until darkness. With any kind of luck, they should be done. The fence from the garden to the barn and the big gate were well started. It would prevent any attackers from riding through the yard and give them a much better defensive position.

Jed knew the Partlow crew would be back soon.

Probably tonight on a hit-and-run attack. He ordered four lookouts posted three hundred yards from each side of the compound. If they saw or heard riders coming, they were to run back to the camp and spread the word. Half of the men stayed on guard duty; the rest slept with their boots on.

Just before dark, Corn McIntosh rode into camp. The cook had beans and bacon and potatoes ready for the crew. Corn ate with them.

"Fer kittenfish sakes, you call this food? Sarah wouldn't feed this to the hogs!" Corn bellowed.

The cook looked up. He was stripped to the waist and had a long scar across his chest. In his right hand, he carried a meat cleaver.

Corn took another bite and grinned. "Course, now, for being on the job such a short time, this grub is mighty tasty. Mighty tasty."

A half hour after supper, Jed had the lookouts posted and the men positioned. Corn motioned to Jed to come outside.

"You know I dabble in politics some?" Corn asked.

"Heard tell."

"Republican state convention comes up in three months. Everett Partlow is scraping up all the votes he can right now to try to tie down the nomination to the U.S. Senate."

"Everett Partlow?"

"Same. Lot of good people want Sam Pomeroy to run again."

"Why won't he?"

"We're working on him. But Ev Partlow is spending money like he grows it on willow brush. He's promising things he can't deliver, sending presents, putting on parties. Right now he's got about half the delegates to the state convention on his side."

"Trying to buy the office?"

"He is. Figures if he gets the nomination, he'll coast in on the shirt tails of U. S. Grant in the general election of seventy-two."

Jed dropped a stone down the open well.

"And you want me to tie Ev Partlow into the Vanderzanden killing quick so he'll be tried before the nominating convention?"

"Sounds like a practical idea, boy."

"Corn, I got another job to do. We're calling ourselves the Sein Valley Cattleman's Protective Association. We got five men's ranches we're fighting for!"

"Jed, I'm thinking about a whole state."

"And I reckon you got an idea how to do this evidence-grabbing against Partlow?"

Corn grinned and spit into the darkness.

"Got an idea or two. You ever hear about some of them doctors during the war who could tell the kind of gun a bullet come from just by looking at it after they dug it out of somebody?"

Jed nodded.

" 'Pears some of them went so far as to say they could tell exactly which gun that lead came from — in some cases. Say a trooper had fallen down and jammed his gun muzzle into a rock. A small burr might get turned inside the muzzle, right on the bore. Then, when that soft lead slug came spinning out the barrel . . .”

“Somebody dug the slugs out of Vanderzanden?”

“Right as corn whiskey, Jed. Old Doc in town did it and I got ’em all. The one that went into his head is the one we’re interested in. There’s a ‘V’ groove in that slug from stem to stern wheeler. Now if Ben’s gun matched . . .”

“That’s a wild, harebrained idea, Corn. Even if it gets Ben, you don’t get Partlow.”

“State attorney said if Ben admits that Partlow told him to kill Vanderzanden, we can try Partlow for murder, too.”

“Whatever you got in mind, forget it, Corn. We just declared war on the Slash S, and they’ll be here with twenty guns before we’re ready. Wish we had one of those new Gatling guns and maybe a cannon or two.”

“Jed, all you got to do is get Ben’s gun, fire a test shot into a box full of rags, and bring me the slug.”

“That’s all? Why don’t you tell me to go over and ask him to confess to murder?” Jed walked around the well.

“You loaned me these men and the cash

with no strings, right?"

"No conditions at all. Just thought you might like to tie up the Vanderzanden killer for sure."

Jed shook his head. "It's too big a risk now. Maybe after we catch Ben red-handed on something else, you can test his iron. It's a one in a thousand bet, and I'm not trying it."

"You expect an attack tonight?" Corn asked.

"I'd guess just after midnight."

"Care if I stay for the fun?"

"Glad to have you if you take that tie-down strap off your six-gun."

"That I can do easy."

Jed turned and went to check his out-posts. It was a habit he had from the war. But he found all four alert and waiting. Each had a rifle and a six-gun. He talked with each man for a few minutes, then moved on. The men never heard Jed come or leave.

It was nearly one a.m. when the guards came in and new ones took their places. Jed made the rounds again. Back in the yard, he climbed the haystack for a better view. He guessed that Partlow would attack from the north. It was masked from the house. Jed lay quietly, listening.

After a long time, he heard leather creak. None of his men was mounted; it had to be Slash S leather. Then, a spur jangled against a stirrup. Jed slid down the stack and ran for the house. He had all of his men ready and waiting in two minutes. Jed took the Spencer rifle and his six-gun and ran quietly for the barn. Wedging against the side of the structure, he looked north.

Nothing. Quiet as a sleeping steer's jawbone. A horse neighed to the east, but the sound cut off abruptly — as if a hand had been clamped over the animal's muzzle.

Jed whispered to the man next to him to pass the word, to watch both east and north.

Suddenly there was no need to whisper. Horses' hoofs hit hard dirt as they pounded toward the dark ranch buildings. Lookouts at the north and east scurried back inside the new fence or past the corral.

To the north, Jed saw a rider distinctly. He rode toward the barn and swerved. Two shots sent his horse floundering under him, and a sudden flare of light appeared as the man touched fire to a torch. The light made a perfect target, and two slugs tore into the cowboy before he could throw the firebrand. It fell to the ground and burned brightly for a few minutes.

That triggered the main attack. Riders flashed past, firing at the house and barn. They tried to find the muzzle blasts of the weapons aimed at them. Two horses plowed into the gate near the corral, dumping the riders. They ran behind the horses, firing. The new fences loomed too tall for the attackers to jump.

Jed followed one rider as he swung past, closer than the others. Jed fired, and the rider toppled from his horse, but a gush of flame burst almost at his feet. A fire bomb! Jed leaped forward to stamp out the flames. Two more men ran up and spattered out a rain of covering fire as Jed stomped the coal oil into blackness before it could soak into the dried-out wood of the barn. The last flames died, and Jed sensed a wetness along his leg. He felt down and it was blood, but it did not seem serious.

"Over here."

Jed heard the plea and saw men running to the haystack. Fire burned at the edges of the dry hay. Two men pulled great chunks of the hay away with pitchforks. Others relayed the hay farther from the fire. It was a race to see who could claim more of the hay.

As the hay blazed up, the attackers pulled back. It had been a token raid, Jed decided, to let him know the Slash S would fight. They could save about half the hay. And the barn would not burn.

It had begun.

Jed picked five men, had them check over their guns, and gave two of them shotguns.

"We're going to pay a neighborly call on the Slash S tonight. But we're not going in like the cavalry charge they made. We're going in like Indians. I'll tell you about it on the way."

Granger stayed in charge at the Double H and put out lookouts. Everyone left at the spread, including Corn, was awake and on guard the rest of the night.

It was after three a.m. by the stars when they pulled up in a clump of cottonwoods along the Sein and rested their horses. It was another half mile into the Partlow spread. Jed outlined it for them once more, then took the shotgun and his pocketful of shells and led the men across the plains at a trot. About four hundred yards from the first corral, Jed stopped and pointed. The men scurried noiselessly to their posts. One man began a slow crawl into the big barn.

Jed carried the shotgun chest-high as he ran from one bush to the next. At last he got the position he wanted. He waited a few moments for everyone to be ready. A match flared at the back side of the door to the barn, and Jed fired one barrel of the scatter gun toward the ranch house. Almost at once guns barked in a wide arc around the Slash S ranch buildings.

At first, there was no answering fire, and when it came, it seemed very light. Jed wondered why.

His answer came from the rear as eight or ten horses rode hard toward them.

"Hold fire!" Jed yelled, and he heard it passed on down the arc of his men. He saw a shadow slip out the rear door of the barn and run toward him. Jed and each of his men crowded into the ground as the Slash S riders thundered past; in the dark the riders could not see their quarry.

As soon as the horsemen swept past, Jed began firing his six-gun again; the others took up the signal. Jed began giving ground as they had planned, firing, running backward, firing again.

The mounted riders organized to make one more sweep across the ground, but before they could get underway, flames from the barn broke through a window, and the alarm drew all available men to fight the roaring barn fire.

Jed and his men jogged back to their horses with no further pursuit. As they mounted, Jed checked out each man. No one had been hit, and all were in high spirits.

"That barn didn't have a chance!" the man who had torched it said grinning. "I found a five-gallon can of coal oil inside and spread it over the hay. It went up like a dead pine tree!"

Chapter Twelve

They pulled into the Double H just after the first false light of dawn shimmered over the hills. The lookouts had moved back inside the fence, and Jed saw two riflemen had replaced the guards.

Corn met them at the corral.

"Did you get Ben's gun? Get a slug for me?"

Jed swung down from his mount; as his left foot hit the ground, the leg folded, and he sat down suddenly. His pants leg below the knee shone wet with blood.

"Awkward of me," Jed said, stumbling up. He limped to the house where Corn cut away the pants leg.

"Just a scratch," Corn jibed at him. "Not big enough furrow to plant taters in." Corn washed out the wound and disinfected it with watered-down whiskey. When he had it bound tightly, Corn snorted.

"Fer kettenfish sakes, I got to ask you

again? Did you get a slug from Ben's gun or didn't you?"

"I didn't, Corn. There was no way without getting killed. Maybe next time." Jed paused. "Corn, were any of those slugs from Vanderzanden dumdum types?"

"Not a one." Corn turned, obviously disappointed. "Think I'll ride into town." He saddled and rode out.

Granger came in, sweat staining the front of his blue shirt. In his hand, he carried some papers, a coin purse, a jackknife, and some odds and ends. He had another stack in his hat.

"We put the two dead men away, Jed. Figured we better save their papers and things. When we get a real sheriff in this county, we can turn them over to him to notify kinfolk."

"Thanks, Granger." He put the effects in two piles. "Send a man out for a yearling. Get anything they can find and haze it back here. Time we had some meat."

Granger moved away quickly, and Jed heard him shout at someone outside.

Jed had half the men on his raid down sleeping — and half the guards. He tried his leg and found it didn't hurt any more to walk on it.

Clint Armstrong came into the dining

room quickly, as if he had to do something before he changed his mind.

"Mr. Hart. I'm quitting. Told you that first day I don't hold to killin'. Two men dead here last night. One man shot so bad his shoulder might never work. I'm going!"

"Sit down, Clint. Time we had a talk."

"I'm packed, ready to ride."

"You get shot up last night?"

"No."

"You shoot anybody with your gun?"

"Don't think so."

"Then your gun didn't do us much good, did it?"

"I reckon not."

"You didn't hold up your part of the bargain for the Sein Valley Cattleman's Protective Association, then?"

"I don't aim to get myself shot for nothing."

"Call that spread of yours and your cattle nothing? So you don't have a house on it. The land deed is still in your name. A man has to stand up and fight for what's right, even if he knows he ain't got a chance of winning. But here we've got a good chance. We got men and money behind us, and we gave worse than we took last night."

"I got a wife and kids. . . ."

"You want to sign over rights to your spread to the rest of us?"

"No, no, never!"

"Then how you figure you can do your share? You want to hire a gun hand to take your place? That'd be fair."

"Can't afford that."

Jed stood and looked out the dining-room window. He would have to take an inspection trip before long.

"Clint, can you cook? You hang your gun on the peg, and you don't have to use it long as the grub's good."

"That'd be my share?"

"Full and even!"

Clint went to tell the unhappy cook he could get out of the kitchen.

Jed heard the heavy report of the rifle before he got outside. He looked down the town trail and saw a lone rider moving at a walk. He came another hundred yards, and a second bullet splattered dirt at the side of his horse. The rider stopped.

Granger jumped on a saddled horse and rode to meet the visitor. As he came into the yard, Jed saw that the man wore no hip holster or gun belt.

He rode erect, tall in the saddle like a major, but his bearing was not military. He swung down from the horse as if he lived half his life in the saddle, but it was plain from the soft features and the whiteness of his face that he was not an outdoorsman.

His eyes were blue and keen, taking in everything. The conservative broadcloth suit shone from wear, but it was clean and pressed. He wore low oxfords, not boots.

As Jed sized up the stranger in the few short strides toward him, he knew the other was doing the same to him. The man was about thirty, and the strong chin was clean-shaven, sideburns high cut, and his nose showed a bend where it had been broken and not healed straight.

"Jed Hart?"

"Right."

"I'm McAbee. Corn McIntosh said you were the man to talk to."

"Could be."

"Could we go for a short ride?"

Ten minutes later, they came out of the brush on the rise behind the ranch house and sat looking down across the spread to Sein Creek and on toward the west.

Neither had spoken. Now Jed turned and knuckled his hat back on his head.

"You're a lawman, McAbee, but I can't figure out what brand."

McAbee took a folded sheet of paper

from his jacket pocket and handed it to Jed.

"I hear you've seen this before."

Jed opened it and saw the message that Harold Vanderzanden had been killed for.

"Vanderzanden was working for me. I want you to take his place. Now, listen me out, Hart. Then you can have your say. There's a cattle-rustling ring in this part of the state that is affecting cattle prices all over the country. They work through two or three cattle-buyers, two big ranchers and a small army of middlemen, and drovers. They steal cattle from trail herds around Dodge City, from as far south as Liberal and back to Wellington and Sumner County. The stock from one end of the area is driven quickly to a distant point and holed up in a secure valley while the brands can be altered and healed. Then they take them the rest of the way to the railhead and sell them through buyers who don't care where they get their beef."

"Mr. McAbee, if this is so big, why ain't folks around here heard something 'bout it?"

"It's small potatoes to any one rancher," McAbee said.

"These boys swoop in and cut out twenty head from a range of two thousand.

By the time the cattle are missed, if ever, it's too late. The rustlers nibble away at a trail drive and pick up five or ten every few days, then move them out, and the drovers can't rightly say how the critters vanished.

"You take twenty teams picking up ten or twelve head a day and it counts up in a hurry. I've got men covering everything else. I'm working the Sumner end. I need a good man here. Corn McIntosh said you were the best."

"You know about the 'Wanted' posters?"

"Yes. Marshal Partlow and his brother Everett are two birds we're trying to snag in our net. The Slash S is the holding and rebranding ranch for the rustlers."

"McAbee, I've already got two jobs. First is to get back the family ranch. Second is to find out who killed Hal Vanderzanden."

"You'll never prove that. I tried. Our lawyers have been over the evidence a dozen times. Without a witness to the shooting, we could never convict. Our lawyers said to give up on it; we'd lose every time."

"That sort of puts a noose around my neck."

"Unless we get the killers for some other crime and they confess to this one, too."

"Like rustling?"

"Right. This is our last chance at Partlow. He's almost ready to nail down the nomination to the U.S. Senate seat. We think he's taking through this last herd, then selling the ranch to his foreman as a front. He'll still control it, but we won't be able to prove it."

"So we got to get him now."

"Right. Where would you hide three thousand cattle for a month around here without anyone running into them?"

"Not in the Sein River valley."

"Remember that old road in back of the Slash S that headed for Coldwater?"

Jed nodded.

"Two miles down that old road is a blind valley. A trail herd should be coming in there within three days. Another herd is due in Sumner County I'll be covering. We need to know when the herd arrives, how many men they have, how many steers. Then we hit them before they can move."

"That doesn't touch Paul Partlow."

"As soon as we nail Ev Partlow, we'll bring in a U.S. Marshal from Wichita, and Paul will be behind his own bars within an hour. After that, we'll send in a state investigator to get the land records straightened out at the county seat."

"Then we really don't need a range war?" Jed asked.

"Right."

"You just signed on a new hand."

"Anything you have to report, make it fast to Corn. If it happens too quickly, you may have to move in yourself. Corn can provide another ten guns for you on an hour's notice."

Jed glanced at the sun. "We'd better get back to the ranch for some dinner."

Granger had kept the men at work all afternoon. They put hinges on the gate, reinforced the fence, and put up log barricades and firing positions every forty feet along the fence. If they had time to dig some trenches, not even Sherman could blast them out.

Jed told Granger about the new change in direction; they would concentrate on holding the Double H and not attack. Granger asked no questions.

About four o'clock, Jed saddled a gray and rode into town. It wasn't quite dark when he got there, and he came into Front Street from the north. He left his horse behind the schoolhouse and slid through the shadows into the backyard of his mother's house. He had watched closely and had seen no one. Still a trace of the old war-time danger surged through him. He forced it down and stepped into the back porch and through the doorway.

His mother lowered the butcher knife.

"Jed? That you?"

"Yes, Ma. It's me."

"Glory, you most scared me into ruin-ation! Be nice when you can come in the front door."

"It certainly will," Emily White said, coming into the room. Her smile sparkled; her long blonde hair was turned up slightly at the ends in a golden crown.

Jed pulled his hat off and remembered he had not combed his hair for days or shaved for at least two days. But he grinned, and her smile came back.

"Miss White, your hair looks a trifle better today than the last time I dropped in."

She laughed, and the special sound was there that Jed had been listening for. Her violet eyes retreated behind blinking lids as Mrs. Hart looked up and laughed softly.

"Well, now," was all she said. But the older woman's eyes brightened, and a smile edged into her weary face.

"You had supper yet?"

"No, Ma."

"Then get washed up some and we'll fix."

"Yes, Ma," Jed said.

"One thing I like in a family, Mrs. Hart, is to see the boys obey their mother. You can tell a lot about a boy just by the way he does what his ma tells him."

Mrs. Hart gave Emily a quick hug before she went to the stove and pushed the pot of stew up front where it was still hot. She sliced two slabs of homemade bread.

Jed splashed cold water into a basin and took it to the back porch and washed.

The food was hot a few moments later, and Jed ate while the women had coffee.

He briefed them on what had happened — the raids on the barn and haystack. He didn't say anything about McAbee.

"Ma, did a letter come for me?"

Emily brought it from the living room. The envelope was plain, the postmark smudged. Jed ripped it open.

"Sister Mary's baby died. Not enough evidence yet to know why. Doctor said too late to worry about that."

There was no signature.

He gave it to the women to read.

"What in the world?"

"What does it mean, Jed?" Emily asked.

"There isn't any legal way to get the

ranch back. The lawyer said he would check it out for us in Coldwater."

The women blinked back disappointment.

"Don't worry, Ma, we've got some other plans cooking." He turned to Emily. "How's that young boy you were so concerned about — Luke Rath?"

Emily covered her face with her hands. "He's fine. Restless, but still in school. I blush every time I think of that! I was so rude!"

Jed laughed and watched her peep through her hands.

"It sure made an impression on me, and I wasn't about to forget you. Here I meet the prettiest girl I've ever seen, and she chews me out like a first sergeant."

Mrs. Hart stood slowly and watched them. "You two go ahead and talk. Just remembered I've got the miseries. Should lay down for a spell." She smiled and left the room.

"Jed, I remembered you since that first day, too. And especially after you scared me when I was washing my hair. If a man can see that and not run away . . ."

He touched the soft blonde hair where it curled along her shoulders.

"Emily, you're the prettiest girl, the

nicest person I've ever met." It was the closest he had ever come to touching her, and his hand came back, weak from the effort.

The front door opened and closed, but they thought nothing about it. Jed wondered what he could say to this girl when the kitchen door swung open.

"Don't move, Jed Hart!" The voice came from an unshaved gun tramp. His clothes were filthy, but the six-gun in his left hand commanded respect.

"Get away from him, woman. I don't aim to splatter blood all over you. Move!"

Emily edged away from the table and backed to the stove.

Chapter Thirteen

"Dead or alive, the poster says," the gunman said. "Partlow wants you alive, but I don't take chances. Get your hands on the table, Hart, palms up!

"Figure I'd always want to call the shots when I get it. How do you want it?"

"How would you like to make five hundred dollars quick money? You're a bounty hunter, why not take more from me than Partlow pays?"

The man laughed.

"Bidding for your skin?" He snorted. "Guess I'd do the same thing, even if I didn't have the money."

"I just took the Double H away from Partlow. I've got fifteen hundred with a friend." Jed saw movement behind the man that he could not believe. It was his mother. She had the two-foot-long ceremonial sword his father bought one day on an impulse. She would get killed!

Before Jed could say a word, Mrs. Hart took two quiet steps forward and lunged. She held the sword at arm's length in both hands and surged ahead with all her weight behind it.

The gunman sensed something behind him and turned halfway to the rear just as the blade reached him. The sword bit into his side and angled upward. It missed the lower rib and knifed into his vitals. The gun dropped from the gunman's hand, and he screamed once before he fell.

Mrs. Hart let go of the handle and stepped back. She weaved a moment and then crumpled to the floor.

Jed spilled his chair backward and lunged for the man's gun on the floor. He had it and quickly checked the gunman's condition. He was almost dead. Only a few drops of blood pooled on the wooden kitchen floor.

"Get Ma's bed ready," Jed said, and Emily hurried out of the room. Jed picked his mother up and carried her into the bedroom. He motioned for Emily to tend her. When Jed got back to the kitchen, the man was dead. Dragging the body by the shoulders, Jed got it out to the back porch. He went back to Emily.

"Take care of her; she just fainted. She

saved my life. If she hadn't come in when she did . . ." He watched a tear crawl down her cheek.

"Was that the first person you ever saw die, Emily?" She nodded, and the tears came freely. She came to him, and his arms came around her. He told her it was all right. He smoothed her hair and talked to her.

"Hold me tight, Jed," she said as the tears stopped. "Every time you ride away I'm afraid it's the last time I'll ever see you. I couldn't bear that!"

He held her close and felt the last tremors of the crying shake her firm body. She pulled back and wiped her eyes.

"I really didn't believe there were men like that one before. Be careful, Jed. Be careful for me!"

He smiled at her, and the swell of emotion was so great in his chest he did not think he could talk. He touched her hair again.

"I'll be careful, and I'll be back. Nothing can hurt me now."

She went with him to the door, looking away from the blood on the floor. She touched his cheek with her hand and smiled past a growing tear as he slipped out the door.

The darkness was complete now. Jed checked the area, but saw nothing unfamiliar. His horse stood fifty yards away. How could he get rid of the body without attracting attention? He decided he could not. If anyone else watched the house, they would spot him for sure.

Jed grabbed the man's arm and leg and lifted the body to his back fireman's style, leaving his right hand free at his holster. The gunman was heavy, and before Jed stumbled to the schoolhouse, he fell, pitching his burden ahead of him. He ran to his horse and led it to the body, steadying the skitterish horse. He picked up the dead gunman and draped him over the horse just in back of the saddle. The gray side-stepped at the smell of death, but Jed held her and stepped aboard. He turned north, walking the gray carefully.

He had his load just past the last house on the north road when a shot blasted from beside the house. Jed heard the bullet sing overhead and touched spurs to the gray's flanks. The horse lunged ahead, and the unwelcome guest slid off onto the road.

Jed never looked back. Two horses spurred from the house in pursuit. He aimed for the Sein Creek trail north toward Buckets Crossing. It was a quarter of a mile to the first good brush. If he could get to that, he could lose one of the riders and jump the other.

The two men behind kept shooting, but the gray had good power and lengthened the gap between the horses at every stride. Jed did not shoot back at them; it was a waste of powder. Just as they crossed a small rise in the valley floor, the men behind fired three shots in quick secession. It had to be a signal, Jed thought. A signal to someone ahead. Jed whipped his horse off the trail to the right and headed into the first cover he could see, a crest of oak trees on a small rise. The pair of riders behind him followed Jed.

If he could get into the rocks above, he could hold off these two and several more. That was when he remembered the shotgun in his saddle boot. The scatter gun could discourage any sudden charge. Jed had the shotgun out of the boot and six shells into his pants pocket when he hit the brush. He dropped off the horse and slapped its flank, sending it scurrying through the trees.

Squatting behind a clump of brush, Jed loaded the shotgun. The two riders pulled to a stop fifty yards away from the trees and listened. They must have heard Jed's horse still slamming through the brush because they spurred after it. They both were shadows in the night, and as they came toward the grove, Jed realized he had to fire before they entered the thicket. The riders closed the range to one hundred feet, and just before they hit the trees, Jed fired.

A shrill scream of pain shattered the night as the near rider fell forward off his mount. The horse charged ahead in panic. The second rider controlled his horse and rode back, looking quickly at his companion before he dug his spurs into horseflesh and headed for the road. The man on the ground did not move.

Jed did not want to go look at the man, but he knew he had to. He knew what a shotgun could do to a man. They are deadly at anything under one hundred feet.

Moving as silently as he could, Jed saw the rider was dead. He reloaded the shotgun and wished the day would come when the killing would end.

It took him a half hour to find his horse. She munched on grass at the other side of the thicket.

Two hours later, he was back at the Double H. The first lookout said there had been no trouble from the Slash S while he had been gone. By the time he stumbled into his old bedroom, he was asleep on his feet. He did not even bother to take off his boots when he hit the bed.

Chapter Fourteen

The smell of frying steak, potatoes, and onions woke Jed the next morning. He rolled out of bed slowly, washed the glue from his eyes at the pump, and grabbed a chair at the table. After eating two steaks and three cups of coffee, he was ready. Jed called the men together around the well.

"How many of you men were in the war?" Several hands went up. "Good, we've got a little scouting job to do, and we need a volunteer."

One of Corn's men stepped out. Jed told Granger to take the rest of the men on his work projects.

"Your name's Harry, right?" Jed asked the volunteer. The man nodded. "You fired the Partlow barn for me, didn't you?"

"That's right. It was a good bonfire."

"Harry, we need to know what's going on at the Partlow spread. We want you to scout it for the next day or two. We want to know everything that happens — when they go out and when they come back, about how many men they have, any new cattle that shows up. Have the cook fix you up with two meals to take along each morning, and stay till dark. Don't use your horse closer than two miles of the spread. Take your time the first day, and find exactly the place you need. Get close enough, but with plenty of cover so they won't spot you."

Jed asked the man to repeat his instructions.

"Be ready to leave in half an hour. If a raiding party heads our way, hightail it back to our first guard. Tonight, come back and report to Granger everything that happened."

Jed talked to Granger and filled him in on what he talked with McAbee about.

"Partlow might be too busy getting this herd moved in and rebranded during the next three or four days to give us any trouble. Least I don't expect any from him. Keep four men on guard at night, two out during the day. I'll be over there for up to three days. If the herd doesn't come in by then, I'll come back for some more food."

Granger said he understood. He pulled off his hat and scratched at his long hair.

171

Drawing his .44 out of his holster three or four times, he then eased it back. At last, he looked up and shook his head.

"I'm not one to talk much, Jed. Jest wanted you to know I appreciate this. You ramroding this thing. Going out after Partlow. Heck, we all should say thanks." He jammed his hat on and strode off toward the barn.

Jed grinned at the stiff back as Granger walked away. He would be a fine neighbor — if they ever got Partlow. He moved to the kitchen and packed a flour sack with food. It had to be a cold camp. No fire of any type to give himself away. He packed enough food to last three days: dried fruit, canned beans, canned peaches, jerky, and hard biscuits. Clint Armstrong fried two steaks for him to take along. The gray was saddled when he came looking for Granger.

"You know everything I know. There's a chance I won't be coming back. But you know what we're trying to do here. If anything happens, see Corn McIntosh. He's a lot more than just a corn-liquor man."

"You'll be back, Jed. We couldn't do it without you."

It felt good to be riding again. For three years, he did little else, not spending much time in any one place. But riding and moving on were two different things. He had no urge to move on this time. He had a strong desire to win this fight with Partlow and to open up the Sein Creek valley to honest ranching again. He thought more and more about that pretty blonde schoolteacher. But he pushed her out of his mind. First had to come Ev Partlow and Ben Matheson. He had a score to settle with both.

Jed turned north again, cut across Sein Creek, and went to the top of the first ridge. From there, he could look down into the Salt Fork Valley. The Slash S was down there, farther west and a little to the north. A finger ridge hid the buildings from sight. He had planned to set up his lookout somewhere along the northern and eastern sides of the valley. That would put him on the far side of the area where men and supplies would come up the old Salt Fork Road from the Slash S. Keeping on an easterly course, he dipped down the side of the slope into the headwaters of the Salt Fork tributaries. Now he was in enemy territory. From long practice, he rode, then halted and listened. When he had stopped in a screen of hickory brush one of those times, he heard a horse running hard.

"Yaaaaaaaa! Hi-yaaaaaaaaaaaaaaa!" The yell of a cowboy hazing cattle came clearly through the clear morning air. Jed wrapped the reins around a branch and stepped softly off the gray. He crawled forward to the edge of the brush and looked out. In the meadow ahead, six men worked a small branding operation. Why branding now? Jed wondered. Then he saw they were rebranding cows. They could have been some local steers picked up by Slash S crews that would join the main herd when it arrived. Jed backed out of the brush and walked to his horse. He led her up the slope until he was sure he was clear of the cowboys. Turning east again, he rode until he came to the edge of the valley he wanted. He knew it was the right one because he could still see traces of the old wagon road that someone had cut along the timber.

At the far side of the meadow, a small log cabin leaned into the wind. There was movement in the cabin, and Jed knew he had arrived none too early. He took his horse a quarter of a mile back from the edge of the valley and tied her after loosening the saddle cinch. He carried the provisions and blanket roll and searched for the best lookout spot.

It took Jed the rest of the afternoon to find the exact spot he wanted. He ate one of the cold steaks and had some biscuits for a quick dinner, then continued his hunt. At last, he found what he wanted. It was directly across from the line shack, well screened with oak and a pair of large cottonwood trees. The spot had been all stone at one time, and the earth had washed away from it, leaving it some forty feet off the floor of the meadow. The only way to get to it was by foot, and it was a hard climb.

Directly in back of the spot, he found a feeder spring, and after digging away a small pool, he had a good spot for drinking. Jed brought the blanket roll and supplies from his cache. He broke off two small branches, and his viewpoint was perfect.

He had seen no security around the cabin and no guards. There was one man at the shack. They were evidently not expecting any action or the whole valley would have been alive with men and guns.

The noise behind him brought Jed rolling to one side, his six-gun clawed from its leather and aimed at the intruder.

The black eyes of a rabbit stared at him for a moment before catching the human scent and scampering into the brush. Jed chuckled to himself to let the nervous tension seep away. The rabbit had scared him more than some of the rebel yells he had heard. He stretched out and watched the valley for over an hour. Nothing happened. He decided there was no value in continual scrutiny, so he moved back into the woods with his supplies and relaxed. He would move up to check every half hour. After clearing a small area of brush and downed trees, Jed set up his camp and rolled out his blanket. He filled his canteen at the spring and took another check on the valley. By stretching, he could see more than half of it. Now two horses stood outside the log-cabin shack, and smoke billowed from the stone chimney. Jed ate the last fried steak the cook had sent and watched a lone wagon pull up to the shack just before darkness. The two men riding in the wagon helped the other two unload it, lugging the goods into the cabin. Lamps glowed across the way as darkness came, and it seemed the visitors would remain for the night. Jed returned to his camp and rolled up in his blanket.

The next morning, he woke, tired and sore. Now his whole plan of attack was to watch and wait. He ate some jerky and biscuits for breakfast, washing them down with cold water. Jed walked back to his horse and moved her, pulling the saddle off. By the time he got back to the lookout, maybe the cattle would be there. But they were not. The wagon and extra men had left, leaving the little valley as deserted as usual.

Jed swore softly and looked at the sun through the tree cover. It was not nine a.m. yet. He went back to his blankets and tried to sleep, but he could not. After staring at the leaves for half an hour, Jed packed a can of peaches and some biscuits in his jacket pocket and started a hike around the lake. He should scout out the far end to see what kind of problems it might show up later.

He stopped when he came to the far end of the small glen. He crawled up to the very edge of the brush and looked it over. The brush was trampled down at one point, as though many hoofs had passed that way two or three months before. This had to be the spot. Only when?

Jed worked back methodically, inspecting the brush for any sign or trail. It was almost four p.m. when he neared his camp. From years of cautious operation,

Jed automatically came up to the big oak tree soundlessly. He peered around it and looked at his camp. Ben Matheson bent over his sack of food.

Jed pulled his .44 and covered Ben as he stepped into sight, twenty feet away.

"Don't move your hand, Ben, or you're a dead man."

Ben straightened slowly, facing Jed.

"So, it's you. We wondered who the new fodder would be to take Vanderzanden's place."

"Now you know. Left-hand that iron out of the holster and drop it into the brush behind you, Ben."

Ben hesitated, and Jed cocked his six-gun. Ben lifted the .44 and threw it behind him. As he did, Jed unbuckled his own gun belt and dropped it to the ground. He let the hammer down easily and tossed his gun to the other side.

"I don't think your fists are as big as your mouth, Ben."

Ben roared and ran at Jed across the open area. Jed sidestepped the lunge and smashed a fist into the big man's kidney as he hurtled past.

Ben turned and advanced slowly. Jed jabbed at him, pounding him on the head. Ben's looping left hand caught Jed in the stomach, smashing the wind out of him. Jed felt himself begin to sag, but before he went down, another fist slammed into his jaw. Jed fell rolling and stopped ten feet down the slope. It saved him for the moment because Ben could not get down the incline to stomp him with his boots. By the time Ben came through the brush, Jed had struggled to his feet.

Jed shook his head, but still the big man weaved in front of him in duplicate. Two Bens moved toward him. Jed blinked again and saw the fist coming. This time it was only one fist, and he ducked it and rammed his own hand into Ben's unprotected jaw. Jed sensed he had hurt him, and he swung his left against Ben's nose, driving him back. Jed circled, gaining the upper slope and charged ahead. His left cracked two, three times into the smashed nose, and when Ben moved both hands to protect his face, Jed rammed his right into Ben's stomach.

Jed leaned into the punch; with the uphill stance, he had gravity on his side. He pounded Ben again in the stomach, and when his hands dropped, Jed swung at the point of his chin and lunged with all the power behind the punch.

Jed heard something snap when his fist

rammed into the solid jawbone, and Ben sagged to the ground and rolled over.

Jed's breath came in surging gasps. His arms hung in front of him, too tired to lift. Both his hands were bruised and beginning to swell. Jed leaned against a tree until he felt sure he could walk; then he hurried to his camp for rope and ran back to Ben. After tying his hands behind his back, Jed used Ben's neckerchief as a gag. He tied his feet securely, then propped the big man against an oak tree and lashed him securely to the trunk, putting the knot at the back of the tree.

Jed's right hand hurt and was swelling. He put it in cold water for a few moments, and it eased the pain. That Ben had found him worried Jed. How did he know where to come? There had been no evidence they could see from the other side. It might have been a security move just before the herd was expected. Since they knew about Vanderzanden, they might suspect he would be replaced.

Jed found his gun and Ben's and moved to the rock for another look at the valley. He heard the cattle before he had climbed all the way. The bawling of tired, thirsty cows drifted down the valley toward him. As he parted the leaves at the lookout, he saw them coming. They entered the valley at the far end, and now the lead animals drank from the stream at the center.

He watched until the red tide stopped coming in the far end. He estimated the herd at about twenty-five hundred.

A chilling thought touched the back of his mind. If Partlow had sent Ben out on a security check, and he did not return when expected, they would come looking for him.

It was time for Jed to move — quickly! He slithered down the rock and grabbed his blanket roll and sack of food. Jed ran quickly, but quietly, to his horse a quarter of a mile back from the valley. He had her saddled when he heard the movement behind him. Jed dove to the ground pulling out his six-gun as the .44 roared in the brush behind him.

Chapter Fifteen

Jed rolled twice, turned and fired by instinct. He could not really say he saw the man. His hand came up, and the weapon went off.

Three times his gun barked and Jed focused on the figure in the hickory brush. The bushwhacker brought his gun up to fire again, but it dropped from his hand; he jolted backward as the heavy .44 slug dug into his chest.

The man was dead, Jed told himself. He jumped up, caught the gray and swung on, sending the horse through the brush, moving due west without looking back. Jed pushed the gray hard for five minutes, looking for the ridge line that would skirt the Salt Fork Valley and bring him around to the Double H. As he topped a small rise, he stopped the horse and let her blow for a minute, looking behind him. He saw no sign of pursuit, and could not hear a sound in the rolling hills.

Jed pushed the gray again. It was six miles to the Double H, and he could change horses there. He had used some of the waiting time to work out exactly what he would do if the cattle arrived. Now he put the plan into operation.

Jed pushed across an open valley and up the other side into the smattering of oak and black walnut. Angling sharply to the southwest now, he rode hard, crashing brush when he had to, but following the small valleys and open ground as much as he could. After another half hour, he was on familiar land and changed his course to due south, splashing across the Sein and heading down the last ridge to the Double H. It was starting to get dark.

The rifle shot came suddenly, and Jed pulled the gray to a walk.

"Sing out who ya are, or you're gut-shot!"

"Hold your fire. Jed Hart."

He pushed the gray forward and soon reined in at the corral.

"Get a fresh horse saddled for me, fast," he called to Granger. Jed ran to the kitchen and poured a cup of coffee from the pot on the back of the ever-hot cook stove. He drank the bitter brew and grimaced.

Jed called another hand in. He was one of Corn's men.

"Want you to ride into town to the Pastime and check to see if Corn's there. If he is, tell him twenty-five hundred head of cattle arrived. He'll understand.

"I'll go to Corn's place in case he's still there." The man saddled a horse and took off for town.

Just before Jed left, he called to Granger.

"Be sure that gray gets wiped down good and give her some oats. She earned it." Granger nodded, and Jed rode out.

Less than an hour later, Jed splashed through the narrows of the creek and charged around the lake. It was dark at the cabin, but as Jed swung down from the horse, he heard a revolver click.

"I'm Jed Hart," he said quickly. Corn laughed.

"Thought it might be. You sure punish a horse." Corn called a hand to take the mount and wipe him down.

"They came, Corn. Must be twenty-five hundred head in there."

"Left Sumner County with about fifteen hundred head," Corn mused. "Must have picked up a few on the way."

Jed went over the story quickly, spelling

out in detail about Ben Matheson and the second man Jed had shot.

"Fer kittenfish sakes, that changes things," Corn said, spitting into the dust. "Take us two days to get a U.S. marshal here or to get McAbee and his men. Partlow must know we're on to him now. He's bound to scatter those cows into the hills and brush, and there goes our evidence."

"Not if we get men and go back tonight," Jed said. "He won't do anything before morning, I'd wager on it."

Corn spat again. "How many men we need to tie them up?"

Jed pushed his hat back. "You got some coffee inside and maybe one of Sarah's pies?"

Sarah caught his hand as soon as they went into the cabin.

"Good to have you back, Jed. Now we get a little class around the joint." She brought him a big piece of pie and a pot of coffee.

They planned it out. The kerosene lantern flickered and the shadows danced as they worked out the details. Corn would go into town and pick up fifteen men. Jed would ride back to the Double H and get all but two of his men there. That would give them about twenty-three men to hold the cattle in the valley and to hit the Slash S.

Corn looked at the dark sky as he saddled his horse.

"Nigh on to eight o'clock. We'll be at the Slash S about midnight with any luck."

"Just hit them fast there and ride on past up that old Salt Fork road."

A few moments later, six men rode out of Corn's place and Jed cut to the right, cross-country to the Double H. He would pick up the rest of the crew at the ranch. His part of the plan would be simple. But could Corn raise enough men in town this time of night? If he did not, if they could not hit the Slash S . . . He would worry about that when and if it happened.

When Jed got back to the Double H, he found them on fifty per cent alert. Harry, the scout, said the Slash S crew were all busy. At least ten new hands had ridden in from the timber. Two wagons were loaded and ready to move out. The whole place blazed with lamps.

Jed called his crew together and told them what had happened.

"Now we ride up there and block the escape hatch because we're closest to them and can get there first. If it looks like they won't drive the cattle out, we'll leave some men and help on the assault on the ranch.

"Any man who wants to can turn in his time right now. There's gonna be some shooting tonight." Jed looked at his crew and especially at Clint Armstrong.

The cook took off his apron and buckled on his gun belt.

"Time I did more around here than burn the hotcakes," he said.

Jed grinned. "We'll take six-guns, rifles, and shotguns. And dig out your extra ammunition. We may need it."

They left ten minutes later. The saddles had been taped and noise-proofed as much as possible. No spurs were worn, no talking allowed. Jed led the nine men along much the same route he had taken the first time, only he swung farther north when he approached the valley. He wanted to be sure to be unheard as they came into position.

They tied their horses in brush half a mile from the end of the valley and moved up quietly. Jed and Harry scouted the valley opening. The cattle had tromped a broad trail through the brush into the meadow. It was twenty feet wide at the narrow point. The men moved from shadow to shadow, checking the end of the opening. The near edge of the herd came within one hundred yards of the opening. They saw only two night herders walking their mounts slowly around the herd.

Jed could only guess why the herd had not yet moved. There was a chance Ben and his friend had been on their way back to town, or on some errand, and had not been missed. Or they may have figured it would take Corn two days to get the state officers here to do anything about the herd.

Granger had started the men filling up the trail with logs, brush, and dead wood. They fronted it with green brush they cut and dug into the ground. It looked like the trail came to a dead end.

Jed positioned men with shotguns closest to the trail entrance. Ten yards around each rim of the meadow, he put riflemen. He sent one man back for his horse so they would have one for quick travel.

The stars showed Jed it was past eleven o'clock. Corn said he would be there around midnight. Leaving Granger in command, Jed took Harry and moved quietly down to his old lookout spot. They came up to it cautiously, but Ben Matheson was gone from the tree. Jed and Harry slid back to the edge of the valley and listened. They edged closer. A cowboy, whistling to himself, walked his mount ten feet from them.

Jed hardly breathed until the rider went past, then lifted his head and looked at the line shack. Light streamed from both windows and the open door. He heard a harmonica and some singing. He thought a bottle was being passed around.

"Doesn't sound like they expect trouble," Harry said.

They moved back into the cover, and Jed asked Harry how far it was from this point to the Slash S buildings. Harry had scouted the area on the first day up here. He said it was no more than half a mile.

"Close enough to hear a pistol shot?"

Harry nodded.

Fifteen minutes later, Jed and Harry found Granger near the blocked trail.

"Don't try to shoot those herdsmen off their mounts, Jed," Granger said. "Those are our men." Granger smiled. "Thought it might be best to take them out of circulation now so we can help keep the stock in place."

Jed laughed. "How did you do it?"

"Pulled a steer over here. When the rider came to haze it back into the pack, we cracked his skull with a rifle. We got both of them tied up over there."

When the next night herder came past, Jed called to him and quickly changed places. Jed walked his horse around the stock. At the far end, he was directly opposite the cabin. Jed saw only four men inside. When he was out of sight of the shack, he spurred back to the end of the meadow and changed places with the first rider and called his men.

"We're going to rush that shack. I saw only four men inside. We might be able to do it with no shooting. If we can, then we'll move on down to help out at the ranch."

Jed pulled one man off his night-riding duties and left one shotgun guard at the trail entrance.

With the six men behind him, Jed moved around the far side of the lake at a dog trot. They paused fifty yards in back of the cabin. Harry went for the Slash S horses and walked them back another two hundred yards from the shack.

Jed and Granger moved quietly up to the door. Each held a shotgun, double-barreled and loaded. They jumped inside the door at the same time, each covering half the room.

"Quiet!" Jed roared, and looked at the five men. Two of them were rolling drunk on the floor, the rest half gone on booze. Granger grabbed their weapons, and the men were hustled outside and tied up in the trees behind the shack.

They heard the rifle shots then, and an answering stutter of hand guns. Corn McIntosh had arrived at the Slash S ranch.

Jed pulled his men along the trail that had once been the Salt Fork road. He put them fifteen yards apart, all on the same side. Nobody could ride through and stay alive. Jed stood at the end nearest the Slash S. He put his ear to the trail and heard hoof beats.

"Hold your fire until I give the word," Jed said. He melted back into the brush and waited.

They knew it was a single rider long before they saw him. The man was small, and in the darkness, Jed could not be sure who it was.

When he was one hundred yards from the cabin, he started yelling.

"Scatter the herd! Stampede them! Get them off my land! I'll be ruined! Move them out!"

Jed realized the man was Ev Partlow. Jed held the shotgun high and moved out to the trail. The rider pulled to a stop in front of him.

"Don't just stand there, idiot!" Partlow said. "Get those steers off my land!"

"Not this time, Partlow. You lose." The shotgun centered on the small man's chest.

"Hart? What're you doing here? Look, I'll give you back your ranch. You can have two thousand head of cattle. Just help me stampede that beef off my range. That's a state man down there. He'll skin me alive!"

Before Jed could respond, Partlow disappeared out of the saddle on the other side of the horse. The frightened animal reared, then pranced away. Partlow hung in the grip of Granger.

He held Partlow with his left and smashed his right fist into the man's nose. His fist slammed into Partlow again and again. Partlow doubled over with the sudden pain from a left into his stomach, and Granger brought up his knee into Partlow's chin and jackknifed him backward into the dirt.

Granger went to his knees pulling Partlow's head up by his hair.

"You probably don't even know me, Partlow. My name's Granger. You burned me out two years ago. You killed my wife. You killed my little girl Sally. You killed my boy Terry. You killed my youngest, Samuel. And you don't even know my name!"

"For God's sakes, Mister, leave me alone!"

"You ever burned to death, Partlow? If I had a match, I'd light your hair on fire so you'd see how it feels!" Granger smashed his fist into the man's crumpled nose again, and his head banged hard into the dirt.

"That's enough, Granger," Jed barked.

Granger's hand snaked to his side, and the six-gun grew in it before Jed touched leather.

"Don't, Jed. I got a heap of respect for you. This is a fever I got to burn out of me. He killed me four times. Now I'm gonna kill him four times! Don't make me kill you to do it!"

Partlow had rolled onto his stomach, his right hand pressed flat against the ground. Granger shot through the back of his hand, and Partlow screamed. He sat up, holding the hand, watching the blood spurt from it. He looked in wonder at the two center fingers that hung limp and useless.

Another shot crashed in the stillness, and the slug tore into Ev Partlow's left knee.

Partlow looked up at Granger. "If you're

a God-fearin' man at all, Mister . . ."

Granger's foot lashed out, smashing his heavy boot into Partlow's face, spilling him backward into the dust.

The man fell unconscious. Granger poured his canteen of water on the man, and he came up gagging and screaming. Partlow tried to stand and run, but his left leg folded. Granger followed him and shot him three more times. Everett Partlow was dead when Granger dropped his six-gun and walked into the brush.

Jed told Harry to use Partlow's horse and to bring up their own mounts. Two men rode away on the horse.

"Men," Jed said. "Partlow is dead, and nothing we can do is gonna help him. Way I remember, he tried to run and a number of us shot. Couldn't tell for sure which slug killed him in the darkness. Right?" Jed took out his .44 and fired in the air, and the other men each fired two or three times.

As their own shots died away, they heard more shooting from below.

"Let's go down and see if we can help out a little," Jed said. He led them on a trot down the trail. They stopped in the heavy grove above the ranch. There had been no shooting for five minutes.

"Corn McIntosh, you down here?" Jed called.

"Course I'm here, fer kittenfish sakes! Think I'm sleeping on the job!" The voice came from twenty feet away in the shadows. Corn laughed.

"It's over down here, Jed. Few got away, but not many."

"We got Partlow. You won't have to worry about him running for any office again."

"Figured he might put up a fight," Corn said.

"You have a few prisoners?"

"Twelve, near as we can count."

"Let's take them down to the jail and throw Paul Partlow in with them," Jed said.

It took almost an hour to round up the prisoners, the dead, and the wounded and get them all on horses. Three men stayed with the herd so it would not stray. They would have to separate the herd into brands and return them to their owners or sell them and return the cash. If any owners could not be found, the Sein Valley Cattleman's Association would have first claim.

The grandfather clock being repaired in the watchmaker's shop beside the jail struck one o'clock as they pulled to a stop in front of Hendersonville's lockup. Corn pounded on the door until the sleepy deputy lifted the latch. He was hustled backward and into a cell before he came fully awake. There were only three cells and twenty prisoners, but they each had room to sit down.

When they were all locked in, Jed rode down the street to his mother's house. He looked up amazed as he saw a light on in the house. Jed spurred his horse the last block and swung off the animal before it stopped. He ran to the door, knocked, and then opened the door and slipped inside. His mother sat in the rocking chair. She had on her nightgown, and her hair was rolled up the way she used to fix it when she went to bed.

She stared at him, hardly seeing.

"What's the matter, Mother? What happened?"

She blinked and then looked at him. "Jed, not an hour ago that Ben Matheson came and made Emily get dressed. He took her away."

Chapter Sixteen

"Ben took Emily?"

"Most an hour ago, Jed. If we'd kept a gun, I could have stopped him."

"Which direction did they go, Ma?"

"Went south — in a buggy. Looked like that little one from the livery."

"You sure they went through town?"

"Headed that way."

"Ma, we still got those miner's lanterns that Pa used to polish? The ones with the big reflectors on them?"

The woman nodded and came out of the chair. She moved purposefully now that she could do something. She found the lantern and filled it with coal oil from a jug. He lit it and let it burn.

"I'll find her, Ma. Don't worry. I'll find her tonight." He shone the lantern into the dust of the road in front of the house, found the fresh buggy tracks easily, then headed south. He trailed them, walking, leading his mount. Halfway to the main intersection, they turned left, then left again, angling north. The tracks were deeper in the land behind the row of houses. Jed mounted and found that by holding the lantern low he could follow the tracks. They angled back toward the schoolhouse, and a quarter of a mile beyond the school, they hit the Sein Creek trail north. Where could Ben be going? Not back to the Slash S? Surely not to the Double H spread. Maybe to Buckets Crossing, or in a roundabout way to get back to the Salt Creek Fork and follow it south into the Indian Territories.

Jed rode hard for a quarter of a mile, then slowed and held the lantern down to check on the wheel tracks. When he found them, he spurted ahead again. They did go to Buckets Crossing, and Jed found where Ben had got out of the buggy and walked around.

The trail turned almost due east from Buckets, and Jed slowly realized this was the direction to Corn's cabin! As far as he knew, the only one at the cabin was Sarah. Corn had taken every man with him!

Jed blew out the lantern, put it beside a tree where he could find it again, and rode hard for Corn's cabin. Why had Ben come out here? Jed could think of only one reason. He must have figured Corn would pull every man out he could. That would leave the home base low on protection. But why kidnap Emily? Jed pondered that as he drove the horse over the dark trail.

At the narrows, Jed tied his horse and walked through the water quietly. He hugged the cliff as it angled toward the cabin and stayed as far away from the lake as he could. He soon came to the trees and slipped through them toward the back of the cabin. He expected no welcoming reception. As he came up, he saw a man sitting on the side steps, a rifle across his knees. His head nodded from time to time. Jed could not tell who it was. Ben could have escaped the trap with another man and arranged to meet him here.

Jed edged against the back wall of the cabin and eased around toward the end where the man sat. He was angled away from Jed, but the slightest turn of his head would betray Jed. He edged closer, step by step, testing each time to be sure some twig wasn't underneath. The guard moved, looked toward the lake, and settled down again. Jed's six-gun was out, and he jumped the last few feet, clubbing the weapon across the guard's head. He moaned softly and crumpled. Jed caught the rifle before it fell. The man was not Ben.

Jed stripped the guard's gun from his belt and stepped onto the porch. It squeaked. Jed had never noticed it before. By the time he had the door open, it seemed to him that everyone in the cabin would be awake.

Ben Matheson was. As Jed stepped into the room, Ben's voice stopped him.

"Far enough. Move slow. This shotgun could go off sudden like. There's a match and a lamp on the table. Light it and step back. Don't try to be a hero. You and Emily White both would get half the buckshot."

Jed's hand shook as he found the match, struck it, and lighted the lamp. He squinted against the new light and saw Ben near the kitchen stove. Emily, behind him, was tied to a chair.

Ben grinned as he exchanged the scatter gun for his .44.

"Thought it would be you, Hart. You and me got some talking to do."

"You ain't got a chance, Ben. Corn and ten men will be here in half an hour. Ev Partlow sang a pretty tune about you."

"You caught Partlow?"

"Got him in a cell block in his brother's jail. He named you in three raiding parties that killed ranchers. He said you shot Vanderzanden."

"That dirty . . . You'll never prove any of it. It's his word against mine."

"Ev says he paid you to do the job, and he's got a 'Wanted' poster about you from Texas that the U.S. marshal is gonna be mighty interested in."

Ben laughed. "Good try, Jed. But I got the gun. Hear you got the sweets about Miss Nice here. No matter — she's my ticket out of here. I'm moving out and taking her with me. She's staying with me until I get into the Territories."

"You won't make it to the door, Ben."

"Arch! Arch!" Ben yelled toward the door. "What you hit old Arch with? You kill him?"

"He'll live. What'd you do with Sarah?"

"Tied her up in the lean-to. Fought like a wildcat. I'm leavin' with this one, Jed. You move a finger to stop me, and I'll slice her face up with my knife. You try to come after me, and you'll find her all used up and thrown out on a trash heap so no man'll want her."

Jed could not answer. The surge of anger and frustration strangled his throat. He jumped toward Matheson, but he was too far away. Ben's .44 clicked as the hammer cocked. Jed stopped, staring at quick death in the black .44 bore.

"Almost wish you'd try it. You've messed me up too much in this town." Ben laughed. "It's a good trade, pretty woman like her for the likes of you."

Jed could think again. Time was what he needed. Corn would be coming out tonight, but when? Bars were closed, but his place stayed open all night. He decided there would be no help from Corn.

"Arch, get in here, you sow-bellied excuse for a man!" There was no answer.

"You probably scrambled his brains, Jed. I'll leave him for you." Ben reached behind Emily and cut the thongs holding her wrists to the chair. She pulled the leather loops off and rubbed her hands.

"Stand up, woman, and get out here in front of me."

"What if I refuse, Ben? What would you do?"

"I'd rip that dress right down to your waist and let you walk around here bare-chested!"

Emily stood slowly and faced him, then moved past him.

His hand brushed her away. "Not between me and that loco cowboy. Back there!"

"Get some grub ready for us. Some of that bread Sarah just baked, and some bacon and all the jerky and dried beans and fruit you can find. Hustle now!"

Emily looked at Jed, and he nodded.

"Better do like the man with the gun says, Emily."

"Now you're making sense, cowboy. Learn to roll with the punch."

"Ev Partlow says you were the one who shot Hal Vanderzanden. Said you gave him that last shot in the back of the head."

"Partlow's a liar! I could tell you a few things about him that'd make your teeth fall out."

"He also said you burned out the Granger place. Said you knew the family was in that barn when you fired it."

Jed saw what Emily was doing. She had started putting food into the sack. As Jed talked, Ben looked more at him than at the girl. She had a heavy iron skillet in her hands.

"Partlow's a liar! He led that raid. Told the men to burn every building."

"You can argue with Partlow about it. Should put you in the same cell."

Emily swung the skillet with both hands.

It smashed into Ben's gun hand and rammed the .44 to the floor.

Jed pawed for his own .44, but before he had it clear of leather, Ben whirled and grabbed the girl and held her in front of him.

"You think that small girl is going to cover all of you, Ben?" Jed asked.

"You won't shoot, Jed. You might hit Miss Nice." He began edging toward the door.

"Go ahead, Jed. I know you won't hit me." Emily said it evenly, but there was a quaver in her voice.

Ben kept moving forward, but Jed did not shoot. Then the decision was out of his hands. Ben shoved Emily hard at Jed and jumped out the door. Jed caught Emily and held her for a second, then surged around her to the door.

For a big man, Ben moved quickly. Jed saw him run around the corral and charge into the woods. He sent two shots after him, then ran. They had to have Ben alive. Jed ran to the edge of the trees, then stopped to listen. He heard movement ahead and ran ten yards toward it and stopped. Ben moved again, and Jed knew he was catching up.

The trees thinned here, and the clouds

scudded away from the moon. Jed saw a large shadow leave an oak tree and slip behind another. Jed moved silently, checking the ground, watching for noise-making sticks.

The last ten feet he charged, his .44 held high. But Ben was not behind the tree. Jed stopped and leaped back as a heavy limb slashed through the air. It hit the tree, and Jed heard Ben running. Jed surged ahead, caught the tiring man on the crest of a slope, and dove for his legs. He caught one, twisting it, and they both rolled down the hill.

Jed got to his feet first and drove his boot into Ben's side. Ben groaned, then was up, catching Jed's leg and pulling him to the ground. Ben swarmed over Jed, pounding him, digging at his eyes with his thumbs. Jed felt himself weakening. He had kept his six-gun out of Ben's reach, but now slammed the weapon against Ben's outthrust jaw. He saw Ben fold up on the ground.

Jed pulled off Ben's neckerchief and tied his hands together with it. He holstered his gun and tried to pick him up. But the fight had drained too much of his strength. Jed hog-tied the big man, fastening his hands to his feet behind his back. Ben would not get away this time.

Back at the cabin, Jed found the cowboy, Archie, still groggy. Emily came out of the cabin and ran to the lean-to with Jed to untie Sarah.

"It's about time somebody came to help me!" Sarah bellowed. "I been tied up for hours."

Jed grinned at her and laughed. "Sarah, I'd like to introduce you to Emily White, our schoolteacher."

"Hi, Emily. Hear you're the smartest, prettiest schoolmarm in the whole state of Kansas."

"Why thank you, Sarah. It's good to meet you."

Jed tied the cowboy to the bunk and herded the women back to the cabin.

The three of them stood in the sudden light of the lamp.

"Is it all over, Jed?" Emily asked.

"Just about — some loose ends."

"The killings all done?"

"Done, Sarah. Done at last."

Emily moved and took Jed's hand. "I'm so glad, Jed."

"Why don't you two sit out on the step where it's cooler while I get some coffee made and see if there's any of the gooseberry pie left," Sarah said.

They had just sat down on the step when they heard hoofbeats coming around the lake. Before the riders were within pistol-shot range, Jed heard the call.

"It's Corn McIntosh, and we're coming in."

When Corn and three riders pulled up, Jed told them about Ben.

"Fer kittenfish sakes! Could have at least waited until we came to help." They all trooped inside, and Sarah dished up the pie and coffee.

"You send word to the U.S. marshal?" Jed asked.

"Should be here tomorrow. I sent a rider about an hour ago."

"What about our land? What can the Sein Valley Cattleman's Association do now?"

"Damned organizers!" Corn said. "I poked around the county clerk's office last time I was over at the county seat. Seems only one title deed's been changed. That was yours, Jed. Granger, Armstrong, and the rest of them still legally own the land they did before Partlow run them off. Just some back taxes to take care of."

"So all they have to do is move back in?" Emily asked.

" 'Pears that way."

"But what about Jed's place?" Sarah asked.

"That works this way. The state can seize Partlow's spread for damages, fines, that sort of thing. The ranch and cows will go up for bid. It'll be advertised and all to make it legal."

"Then anybody could come in and buy the ranch and the Double H spread, too," Emily blurted.

"Right, ma'am. 'Cept after I get through making my little talk before the auction, I don't reckon nobody will want to bid on the place 'cept Jed."

Jed shuffled his feet on the rough wooden floor.

"Corn, we don't want nothing but what's ours. If that's the way we got to do it, I bet the rest of the Slash S would go up for sale mighty cheap."

There were some heads nodding round the room. Then Jed looked at Corn again.

"You see Granger?"

"Heard about it. Man like him needs to sort things out after something happens. He's bound to be back in town in a few days."

"Think I better get Miss Emily back home and tell Ma she's all right. I won't have her worrying any more."

Outside, a few moments later, Jed turned back to Corn.

"Think you can talk Senator Pomeroy into running again?"

"No problem 'tall. Not when he hears about Partlow. He'll run like a greased polecat across a hot rock."

"Corn, you never did tell me how you got so close tied in with the state people. You really a colonel in the state militia or something?"

Corn sent a squirt of black juice into the night and chuckled.

"Nope. I'm mostly what I seem to be. I make good corn whiskey. Grew up with Pomeroy, so I'm partial to old Sam. He asked me to see what I could do to help this rustling thing. I just sent the letters on. Don't even rightly know what McAbee's real job is."

He looked at Emily and back at Jed. "Boy, if I was only sixty again, I'd give you a run for your girl!" They all laughed, and the silence stretched out.

"Most forgot to tell you, Jed. There was a reward out for that rustling gang. Two dollars a head for the cattle returned and a thousand dollars for every rebranding ranch. You'll be getting some cash from his honor James M. Harvey, our fine governor."

Corn had sent a man to bring the buggy up from where Ben had hidden it. When it came. Jed and Emily stepped up in it.

"What're you going to do with Ben?"

"State will want him on the rustling charge. He should get at least twenty years if they don't hang him."

Jed waved at him and slapped the reins against the horse's back.

Just beyond the narrows, where the prairie gave way to the gentle foothills, Jed brought the buggy to a stop.

"It's time I got one more thing straightened out," Jed said, looking at Emily sternly. "I think you should quit teaching school."

"Why, Jed?"

"What I mean is, I'm not going to move out to the Double H ranch alone, and it would be a long way for you to drive in every day. And besides, I won't have a wife of mine working."

"Oh, Jed, I'll be glad to quit teaching school!"

Jed tied the reins and clucked to the horse. It knew the way back to town, and there was no hurry.